D1607815

BIG BAD
Wolfe

USA TODAY BESTSELLING AUTHOR

SUSANA MOHEL

Big Bad Wolfe by Susana Mohel

Editing: Alexia Chase Romance

Proofread: Ariadna Basulto

Cover picture: Xram Radge

Cover model: Gleiderson R Gasparrini

Love her but leave her wild.

—Atticus Poetry

CHAPTER 1

London

Things are going downhill. Like in a biblical sense, right down the damn hill. Or more like a mountain.

Fuck, fuck, fuck.

I land with my foot lodged into a place I can't escape, and everything hurts.

What's happening here? I fight to get my foot out of the hole. This hole wasn't made by an animal. What is this, a trap? Sharp barbed-wire cuts into my skin, every movement becoming more painful.

How the hell did I find myself in this position? I'm going to die here on a mountain where no one will look for me. With my luck, I'll probably be eaten by a bear. Tears sting my eyes. *Do something. Think of something. You're not dying here.*

My boss said this would be an easy job. Just go, knock on his door, and make the infamous Preston Wolfe sign the contract they sent him yesterday via email. I currently have a printed copy of said contract tucked in my satchel.

My plan was simple.

My boss, Mr. McCain, said Preston Wolfe is a prick, but he also can't resist a good pair of legs, such as mine. He suggested I wear a miniskirt to sweeten the deal, ensuring he signs. I had no intentions of failing during my first week at my new job, so I took his suggestion and dressed the part. But nothing is going as planned.

First, my stupid car broke down, forcing me to take a detour on foot. Then, half of my leg is stuck in a hole, aching like you wouldn't believe. On top of all that, my phone is dead.

Now, I'm in the middle of nowhere, praying for a miracle. Hoping some hikers are around, ready to come to my rescue. Even better if they're handsome, single, good with kids, and emotionally available. Oh, I can't forget, they must be able to hold a job. I'm not into leeches. Nope, move on, thank you very much.

I can't deal with anything else. My new job is shitty, but I need the commission from this signed contract to pay for my brother's hospital bills. Right at this moment, it's not looking like I'll accomplish my damn mission or survive the night, for that matter.

I'm not a mountain—or forest—kind of gal. I love life in the city: the lights, the restaurants, the shopping. Until a few months ago, my life was what every girl would dream of. Landing a great job right after graduating from an Ivy League school, a dreamy boyfriend, and a beautiful apartment. The dream didn't last long.

First, my brother got sick, and I missed work to take care of him. In turn, my boss wasn't happy about my erratic attendance, which caused me to get fired from said job. Then I found out that my dreamy boyfriend—now ex—fucked my so-called best friend. Therefore, causing me to move out of my beautiful apartment. With my brother needing my help and my urgent need for an affordable place to live, it just made sense to move in together.

I scoured the web for a position with flexible work hours and applied to many different places, hoping to find something quick. An offer from Western Woods came my way, and it was impossible to refuse. They offered me an hourly rate, plus a commission for getting contracts signed.

My brother is doing better, so a short road trip should've been a cinch to earn that first commission - getting Preston Wolfe to sign this contract.

Wolfe's property is in the middle of California, surrounded by mountains. It's an area covered with trees, the perfect place for a company like Western Woods to expand its operations. But WW isn't the only company trying to purchase the land from Wolfe. However, WW came with a solid offer to seal the deal.

Why in the living hell didn't I call for help? Why did I take this stupid shortcut and not follow the small winding road, leading directly to the main house? Google maps said I was walking in the right direction to the property, but the damn app didn't say a word about human traps. Some help they are.

It's past four in the afternoon, soon, it'll be dark, and I'm pretty sure if I'm stuck out here all night, I'll be eaten by an animal, perhaps even a wolf. Not the end I had in mind. Far from it.

I close my eyes, trying to remember how to pray, when suddenly I hear a snapping sound. I open my eyes and freeze in alarm.

More rustling causes my heart to pump hard against my ribs. I yank my cell phone out. Shit, my phone battery is dead, but it's not like I can call anyone to ask for help, anyway. Frustrated, I toss my phone to the ground. I scan the trees, looking for what's making the noise. And an escape route, not that I can move.

"Look what the cat dragged in," a masculine voice says at my back.

My eyes widen as I turn my head and catch sight of a man. My mouth goes dry, and my throat tightens as my heart almost stops beating.

"Who are you?"

Sunlight glints through the trees and a pair of steel-gray eyes stare at me with a lethal look. He's in jeans, boots, and a Henley. His forearms rippling with muscles.

The man is wielding a gun, pointing it directly at my head. *Fuck.* The situation I've found myself in is becoming direr by the second.

"Hey," I stammer. My eyes are glued to the gun. *Breathe.* "Wait a second, I'm London Moore. I'm here because—"

"What are you doing out here, little Red?"

"Excuse me?"

The man frowns and moves closer to me. God, he's gorgeous. Under different circumstances, I would be ready to bat my lashes and wait for him to ask for my number.

He doesn't reply, just cocks the shotgun. I gasp.

"You're trespassing on my land."

"You're Preston Wolfe," I declare, realizing who he is.

His eyes narrow. "You admit it. You know who I am?"

"Yes," I reply. "I mean, I'm here to talk with you."

"Of course, you are," he says. "Trying to trick me to steal my land."

"No," I inform him. My heart thundering in my chest. "You see, my car broke down, and I thought taking this detour was a good idea. Then I fell into this trap.... Can you help me to get outta here?"

"No," he says. "You know trespassing is illegal in this state?"

"Help me get out of here!" Is he going to let me die here?

I'm rewarded with a smirk.

"If that's your way of asking for help, miss. You're fucked."

"Please?"

"I'll think about it."

I groan in frustration. He's impossible. "What in the fuck do you want?"

"Such a dirty mouth on a beautiful girl."

"I would be nicer if I weren't in pain with my foot stuck in this trap with a dickhead pointing a gun at me."

The man smirks again. But he lowers the gun. Thank goodness.

"I'm not here to steal anything. I'm not a thief. I'm a Western Woods employee."

"Same shit," he scoffs. "They even sent you here wearing a short skirt."

He scratches his bearded chin, his gray eyes assessing me from head to toe, leaving me aroused, knowing that I shouldn't be. The sunlight filters through the canopy of trees above us, making him look like a god.

Jesus Christ, the man, is so freaking hot. It should be illegal. The sanity of the female population around him is at risk.

I groan under my breath. My lady bits shouldn't be taking notice, considering the situation I'm in. My damn libido is messing with me because I'm actually checking out the rugged mountain man, despite the pain I'm in. It doesn't matter how hot he could be. Right?

Preston finally steps toward me, which makes my pulse beat even faster.

"Don't move," he orders.

While he kneels beside me, I study his thick dark hair and the fullness of his lashes that most women would pay a fortune for. His hands move over my bare thigh below the hem of my skirt. The pads of his fingers are rough, causing my skin to tingle. I shudder as those hands slide down my leg toward my getting-worse-by-the-minute swollen ankle.

Preston Wolfe reaches into his jeans and pulls out a pocket knife, which he uses to slip through the trap. The wire around my ankle loosens, and acting on impulse, I yank my leg free, whining as the back of my ankle catches on the barbs.

"Thank you," I say through gritted teeth. I turn, hobble over, picking up my phone and bag.. While trying to stand back up, he grabs me and tosses me over his shoulder. Caveman-style.

"What the fuck?"

Preston Wolfe carries me as if I weigh nothing and then begins to walk. It doesn't matter to him how loud I'm screaming or how hard I'm pounding on his back. He's all muscle. I feel like an ant fighting an elephant.

"Let me go, you big brute!" I snap, still hitting him with my fists as if they were hammers. "You big ape, let me go!"

"I'm trying to help you, stubborn girl. I need to check on that ankle of yours," he scolds, his hands tightening around my body as he starts to walk down a path through the thick tall trees.

"I don't need your help!" I cry out loud. "I can take care of myself. Let me go, right the fuck now!"

Of course, he's not heeding my words. He's focused on traipsing through the forest with me over his shoulder and the gun in his hand.

"Let me go!"

"No," he says. "I haven't decided that you aren't here to trick me. I need to keep an eye on you."

An eye on me? What does that even mean?

"Are you kidding me?" I question unbelievably. "Fucker."

"Do you think I'm kidding?"

I wiggle in his hold.

"Are you fucking kidnapping me?"

"That little mouth of yours will get you in trouble, Red," he snarls. His voice is like thunder, shaking me.

"Red? Seriously?" What a bossy prick.

He doesn't say a word, just slaps my ass as if he has every right to do it.

I shiver, his unexpected action like a wave crashing over me, making me drown in my arousal.

"I'm not here to trick you. I'm here from Western Woods. My boss wants to offer you a fair deal with a substantial amount of money in exchange for your land!" I yell, trying to make him understand.

Preston comes to a stop. A low growl rumbles through his chest. When I gasp, he pulls me off his shoulder and shoves me up against a tree.

"What do you really want?" I swallow the hard lump in my throat. Why does that question in that deep timbre sound like an indecent proposal? I think I made a terrible mistake coming into the lion's den. Or should I say into the wolf's den?

"Western Woods, you know? The reputable company, who's offering you an amazing deal…."

"I know who they are." His eyes flash with anger. "I know who sent you here. I don't care if they branded the fucking company with a fancy as shit name. Shit will always be shit."

I gasp at his words.

"Do you think anything happens on this mountain without my knowledge? You didn't come out to *ask* me to sign a deal. You came out to try and trick me." He snarls the words out, narrowing his gorgeous eyes on me.

"Mr. Wolfe…"

"Look, miss…" he scowls as if he doesn't remember my name.

"Miss London Moore," I say, tipping out my chin. I'm trying to remain composed. Well, as composed as you can be in a situation like this.

"I take it all back then, London." Preston smiles, but it doesn't reach his eyes.

I sigh, feeling defeated. And frustrated. "Thank you. Now, as I was saying…."

He looks at my hair, then at my naked legs.

"You're dangerous…." That sounds like an accusation.

"Wha—" My breath catches as he throws me over his shoulder again and begins to walk. My heart is hammering hard against my ribs like a drum.

"Put me down, Preston Wolfe. I don't want to go anywhere with you. You don't have any right to manhandle me this way." I'm a liar. A fucking liar. Good thing my nose doesn't grow like Pinocchio's.

"You're mine now," he growls. Lust curls low in my belly. Don't go there. Don't be stupid. He's a prick. It doesn't matter how sexy he looks. Or sounds. Or how sinful it feels to bounce against him.

I'm not giving in without a fight.

"What did you say?" I ask breathily.

"I knew you were one of them."

"What are you talking about? I'm just here to…."

"To kick me off my land, right?" he growls. "But whatever you are, you were trespassing on private property. And now, I'm going to punish you."

Punish me? A dangerous thing inside me is screaming *yes, please.*

CHAPTER 2

Preston

The beast living inside me is already howling.

This is going to be fun.

Most women, when in my presence, are ready to do whatever it takes to get into my bed.

But this woman chooses to fight back, to argue with me, and there's no use in pretending she doesn't affect my libido.

She makes my blood boil.

My cock is so fucking hard.

Something like lightning bolts through me.

My chest rumbles as I stalk out of the woods to the main road up to my house, her tight body squirming against me. Hell and damnation, I've been on this mountain way too long because I'm acting like a fucking teenager, getting a boner over this temptress.

Her hair looks like fire, one that's igniting a flame inside me.

Her legs go on for days. Up until today, I thought I was a breast man. But after one look at her in that miniskirt and those legs, I was a goner. I can't wait to have those long limbs around my waist while I pound into her.

Even though I want to mess with her body, I must remember, she's here for my land. But first, I need to check that ankle. I may be a mountain man, but I'm not a hermit. I still know how to act like a civilized human being.

I have some amenities at the cabin, and all that is mine is at her disposal.

My mind runs at the thought of that beautiful body naked in my tub covered in suds.

I want to run my hands all over that soft skin.

She's sassy and feisty; I can't wait to discover how fun it would be to have that fire burning up my bed sheets.

She hasn't stopped fighting me or trying to slap her way free the entire way back to my house. She's like a wildcat for me to tame.

While gazing into her green eyes, I saw the honesty shine through. I kind of believe her when she says that she's not here to trick me. But then again, I can't be too careful. Either she is telling me the truth, or she's a damn good liar.

The second she told me who she was, I knew she was here with a contract to take my land. To leave me with nothing.

I want to believe that she genuinely thinks she's working for a wood trading company. Otherwise, I don't know what a girl like her is doing working for a fucker like McCain at Western Woods. WW is a façade company. A front. It's who they really are that has me so angry.

When dealing with these fucking kinds of people, it's like dancing with the devil. You'll get burned—or it'll get me killed. I'm beginning to second-guess myself. She might be dressed like a lawyer or some shit, but she could be a spy. Hell, she might've stepped in that trap on purpose just to draw me out so I could find her. A pretty thing like her? Fuck, makes any man—me—think she was hand-picked to seduce him.

Not necessarily hand-picked by Western Woods. But by the McCains.

Have you ever heard of Shakespeare's famous love story? Two families that got into one of the bloodiest family feuds in history… Well, we're worse. Way worse.

This war was declared eons ago. Death will not end it. There are no gunfights in the middle of town at noon or any of that shit, but the rivalry is there. It's the Wolfes versus the McCains. After serving in the Army, the only thing I crave is a quiet life on the land that has been in my family for generations. One day, this land will belong to my kids and so on. That's the main reason I don't plan on selling, let alone to the McCains, who are nothing but a bunch of cons.

I have an organized and productive business here. I would never want my land to be used for anything illegal. Even if it's legal in this state, growing weed isn't my thing.

I've heard that the McCain family has their hands in lots of pots. All questionable, but definitely criminal. I despise those fuckers. Western Woods is a fake front they set up a few months back. They know that real wood trade companies are out there looking for big land like mine because it's close to access routes. I know why WW wants this land. The McCains want to turn this property into a huge pot farm, an illegal grow-op. Those fuckers want to strip mine the land and leave us dealing with the ruin.

At least part of it, because they would need to keep up the façade. The part they want to keep in control of, so they can keep running their drugs and meth, or whatever they're up to throughout the mountains without alerting the authorities.

I don't know how the fuck she fits into all this, but I knew the second I saw her that she was trouble. Right now, trouble is looking real good.

"Let me go, you fucking asshole. Put me down!"

Her movements get wilder as I step up onto my porch. She somehow gets a knee into my ribs, but I ignore it. She's small compared to me.

Gorgeous.

Sexy as hell.

And fuck, the mere scent of her across my face has my balls aching and my cock engorged.

Her milky skin is sprinkled with freckles. Cream and caramel, a mix I've never been a fan of before. Now, my mouth is salivating. I want to run my tongue across her body and discover where those paths go.

Fuck, why am I lusting like a teenager after the enemy? The one who wants to help those people take my land?

This land is never leaving my family, and it sure as fuck isn't going to the McCains or any other company for that matter. I should call the police and get him to throw her ass in the lockup for trespassing. Let someone else deal with her and her injured leg.

But here I am, stepping into my cabin with her. This is literally welcoming the enemy in.

The door slams shut behind me, and I storm into the living room, toward my couch.

London's squirming and shrieks suddenly turn into something else.

"Please don't hurt me!" she cries. "I won't tell anyone about this. Please, Mr. Wolfe… I… I…"

I toss her down onto the couch and roll my eyes. My gun is in the waist of my jeans, her enormous purse still in my hand. What does she have there?

"You think if I was that sort of man, I'd bring you all the way down here to my house just to fuck you on the couch?"

London's mouth purses into a thin line, her wild green eyes darting daggers at my face.

"Sit and stay still."

I drop to my knees and go for her leg, but she suddenly kicks the hell out of me with her uninjured leg.

Fuck. She's strong.

I grunt, seeing stars as her foot catches me square in the jaw. I blink, lurching for her until the sudden sound of a shell being chambered has me stopping in my tracks. I shake my head, clearing the spots and the stars to see her standing right in front of me.

"I'm leaving now," she hisses, her face stormy but scared, her deep-green eyes still darting all over the place.

"London…"

"Don't dare to come any closer!" she yells at me.

"Damn," I hiss, whirling back to her and growling. "I'm trying to help you with that ankle…"

"Don't dare to put your hands on…"

She blinks, and suddenly, it's like the fight goes out of her. As if I cast a spell on her.

Well, maybe, because I'm feeling the same way.

God, she's gorgeous.

But there are more urgent matters to tend to.

My eyes drop to the raw redness of her ankle, where she was caught, and I swear under my breath. Fuck. The blood is still fresh, which means she must have nicked one of the tipped barbs right before I got her free.

"London," I growl, my hands steadying her as she sways, blinking up into my face. "You need some rest. You're tired and hurt. Let me run you a bath."

"Are you trying to get me into bed?" she whispers.

If she only knew…

"Not like that. I want to make you feel better and safe…." I say with a shake of my head.

"You kidnapped me, and now you want me to feel *safe?*" she asks in disbelief.

This girl is strong. I love the fight in her. I can't wait to feel her fighting me… between the sheets of my bed.

"Take it easy, Red," I order, catching her in my arms. "I want you to calm down, or you're gonna make your leg worse."

"Don't dare to touch me." Her breathing is more labored, and I can see her pupils dilating.

Oh, her thoughts are absolutely on the same wavelength as mine.

As much as I want to give in to our attraction, there's something about her that makes me need to put her well-being first. I have to check on her injury. She needs to trust me. Otherwise this won't work. A woman like London deserves to be pampered and cherished. I'm here, ready to deliver when the time is right.

Every time I glance at her, I get hotter.

Fuck, I couldn't imagine it would feel like this. Having her in my arms like this… feels perfect. But if they sent her here and she doesn't return, they will be coming to get her. This is a shitty situation, a clusterfuck. I need to call my grandfather and gather all the information I can get.

And I plan to do that while London soaks in my huge copper bathtub.

She's the messenger, and I'm smart enough to know, they are using her like a pawn, a weapon against me. I must remember that.

This was a smart move on their part, but it also reveals how much knowledge they may have about me. London is exactly the kind of woman I would normally go for. Any red-blooded male would. Beautiful face, perky rack, and legs to die for.

Especially how her sweet body felt in my arms as I carried her inside my cabin. Fuck, I'm doomed. There is no way I can let her go.

The way her eyes opened while looking around my room—soon to be *our* room. Yes, maybe I'm acting like a savage, but I don't care—she will be mine. I have plenty of money in my bank account and the brains to manage it. I can afford to keep her here in my oversized soft bed with thick fluffy blankets, provide her with hot water to bathe in, and a fireplace to keep her warm.

"Wait here." I place her in one of the big leather chairs in front of the fireplace. "I'll fill the tub for you."

My voice is low and soft, soothing her.

With time, she will learn to trust me. She's safe here, but I also need to figure out what my enemies have planned next. It won't end here. They'll make every attempt to take my land by any means necessary.

I'm positive it's gonna be a big problem. The kind of problem that comes with lots of men and weapons.

If they want war, I'll be ready and waiting.

But first, my girl needs to eat and rest.

I take one last look at her over my shoulder before entering the en suite bathroom. She looks perfect, like she belongs right in my home.

Now I need to figure out what to do to make her stay.

Forever.

CHAPTER 3

London

After the day I've had…. This is heaven, and I never want to get out of this tub. EVER.

The entire room—and the cabin—is like a dream. Including the owner. The space is modern and clean. For a man who is known for being a savage, this is beyond luxury.

I wonder who the real Preston Wolfe is, the beast or the gentleman—maybe a mix of the two.

My imagination is running wild, and Mr. Big Bad Wolf is the main character in my fantasies. My hands travel along my wet skin, and I imagine they're his.

His hands are everywhere while his mouth hungrily drops to my neck, biting and sucking. I writhe and moan in pleasure as the warm water around me sloshes over the side of the tub and ends up on the floor. He's making me hot like an inferno, even submerged, it can't be doused. I've lost control under his rough fingers, and when he touches me, I burn. I cry out as his fingers push inside my slippery pussy.

"Time to show you who's in charge," he growls, and then adds, "I'm going to show you what I do to little girls who wander alone around the forest."

I want to tell him again that I'm not one, but a part of me doesn't want to. The part of me—my alter ego, I guess—wants to know how he punishes the people who would ever dare to trespass on his property.

"Perhaps, I'll just take you to my bed, tie you up and fuck you hard. I promise I'll have you screaming and begging for more before I let you come all over my cock—if I even allow it."

As my eyes close, a moan escapes my lips. His filthy words and promises make my entire body ache and my blood scorch like an uncontrollable fire. He flips me over the edge of the tub and pins me down. His knees go to either side of my thighs with his hand at the small of my back. The other, grips my tangled hair in a tight hold, making me gasp. He pushes his hips forward, and heat emanates from the throbbing head of his cock easing between my cheeks. He moves forward, gently gliding through my slick center, between my eager lips, right to my clit, and I detonate, his movements making me explode.

And I come. Hard.

My heart races because of my *wet* dream, and the slick heat between my thighs is something I can't ignore. I gasp quietly. The vividness of the dream is still simmering throughout my body. A tingling runs over my skin as if this was real and he's here with me.

I open my eyes and come face to face with Mr. Big Bad Wolf himself. His eyes burn me with an intensity—better to see me with—his penetrating gaze has me pinned in place, solely focused on my naked body.

The fucker was watching me while I took care of myself.

And orgasmed while I fantasized about him.

I'm currently on display in front of a man I don't know, who caught me in a trap, then carried me to his home in the middle of the woods. I should be more concerned about my predicament. As he offers me a wicked smile that shows off his pearly whites—better to eat me with—knowing how surprised I am to have been caught again.

Now all I can think about is him devouring me, with his eyes, with his teeth—with just about anything. Why am I so horny? I should want to escape him.

My heart jumps into my throat, my pulse racing as I start to freak out. I don't know how to respond. I want to slap him, and at the same time, I want to kiss the fuck out of him.

And the thought of him tying me to his bed… why am I overheating?

He clears his throat, and it snaps me out of my reverie. I see him standing in the doorway to the bathroom, coffee in one hand. I blink, my mouth going dry as I struggle to get my bearings.

"You had a good one there," he says, a smirk pulling his lips up.

My eyes drag up his body, now covered in a thermal white t-shirt pulled tight across his bulging arms and strong chest. The bottom half of his body is covered in a pair of jeans and boots. I stop at his smug, grinning face, and I glare. Cocky asshole.

"Do you spy on all your guests, Mr. Wolfe?" Anger surges through me, mixed with a heavy dose of lust. The first, I understand. The second, has me feeling weak and off-kilter.

Preston shrugs. "You aren't my guest," he growls. "You're a trespasser, so I could do whatever I want with you."

"What? How? That's not possible."

"The sheriff or his deputies don't come to this side of the mountain. My land. My rules."

My eyes narrow at him. "That's ridiculous," I spit out before I glance down at myself. "Seems like being a perv is your thing. Now, if you'll excuse me, I'll be leaving."

Preston chuckles.

"And how are you planning on doing that?" He moves toward me, and I swallow thickly. "Your car overheated and doesn't work. I won't let you wander around the woods alone at night. It's too dangerous for a woman like you."

I blush, but something inside me ignites. "A woman like me? What does that even mean?"

He ignores my question. "And maybe you'd want to recover your clothing before venturing outside the cabin, am I correct in my assumption? But before we discuss you leaving, shall we talk about what you were thinking about during your soak. It was me, wasn't it? Me making you feel good?"

My face goes crimson while I take a towel from the rack. Acting as if I don't have a care in the world and securely wrapping it around my body.

"I wasn't thinking of you." I vehemently state, as if I believe my own lie.

He smiles.

"Sure, you weren't. Like that wasn't my name, you were moaning out loud." He dons an even cockier smile.

I cringe. Earth, could you swallow me up right now? Pretty please.

He walks further into the bathroom as if he owns it—well, he does, but it's currently occupied by me—leans close, right over me. I gasp, wondering if he's about to devour me like

I imagined. But his lips graze beyond mine, brushing my cheek until they reach my ear.

"You ask nice enough, and I just might do what you dreamed of, little Red," he purrs as my entire body shivers in delight.

"What are you doing?" I swallow, panting. "You're a freaking villain."

"Yeah?" He chuckles deeply. I hold my breath. It's all I can do to hold back my whimper. "Looking awfully flushed for being so appalled by me, London."

"If you're meaning…."

"Do your pretty little nipples always get hard as diamonds when you take a bath? That can't be comfortable."

I balk, my jaw dropping as I stare at him in shock. But he ignores my reaction and continues.

"I watched you getting off. I listened to you moaning my name too," he growls. His gorgeous gray eyes caress me as if it's a physical touch. "It looked as though you had an earth-shattering climax."

"What I was doing is none of your business. This may be your house, but my body is mine, and mine alone."

"Right. Whatever you say," Preston says sarcastically. "You weren't thinking about me. I must've been hearing things when I heard you moaning my name. And I'm sure I didn't see you grinding your hips like someone was fucking you hard and giving you everything you wanted."

I must look like quite a sight at my obvious embarrassment. I can barely even comprehend how he's talking to me looking this way. I know I should hate it or be wildly offended. But I'm not; not even close, quite the opposite, actually. No one's ever talked to me like this, and good Lord, it does things to me.

"I'm sure I just made that all up," he growls. "Like I'm sure if I lift that towel and run my hands up those pretty thighs and between your legs, finding your sweet little pussy all nice and hot and wet, it would all be make-believe too, right?"

My jaw drops, and I gasp at his forwardness.

There's a second where we both just stare at each other. The undeniable chemistry crackles between us.

"Do you mind leaving, jackass? I need to get dressed."

"Not at all."

"Leave me alone!" I spit out, exasperatedly.

"Tell me who you work for first." He gazes intently, awaiting my reply.

"I already did," I mutter.

"I want you to tell me again."

I sigh. "I work for Western Woods, and I can promise you that we'll be pressing charges for—" He cuts me off from continuing my threat.

"Who do you really work for?"

I stare at him. "Are you like, touched or something?"

"Are you volunteering?"

Heat burns my cheeks. "No. I mean, are you touched in the head, like a crazy person?"

"People will say anything when they're backed into a corner. So, I'm going to ask you once more, and you're going to look me in the eye and give me an honest answer."

He gives me a look with a lifted brow.

"Who do you work for?"

"Western Woods," I reply.

Slowly, he nods. "Well, okay then." He starts to walk away, and I stare at him.

"Wait, just like that?"

"Just like that."

"Control freak asshole," I mutter.

Preston turns back and eyes me. "What did you say? Something about control? I can always finish what you started if you want me to take charge."

I purse my lips.

"Or you could have coffee."

I give him the stink eye, biting back the words I want to throw out, but the coffee mug in his hand tempts me almost as much as he does.

"Coffee."

"Say please." He orders.

"Coffee, please," I grumble.

"See? Up here in the mountains, even beasts, like me, have manners."

As he's passing me the coffee, I swing my arm wide, knocking the steaming mug out of his hand and into his chest. Preston howls, and I shove him aside, causing him to stumble. With the first step, pain shoots through my leg. Fuck.

I hobble down the hall, not caring that I lost the towel I was wrapped in. He's chasing me, and I hear his footsteps thunder closer. And then, he's there. His heat scorches my back. When he tackles me, I scream. We both fall, crashing and tumbling down to the floor. Both of us grunting as we hit the hardwood planks. I blink, my head spinning and my vision blurring for a moment before I realize that we're face to face, and I'm laying right on top of him.

And I can feel every inch of him grinding against my bare core. There is nothing more than his jeans separating us.

We're panting, both of us inches apart. Eyes wild and lips almost touching. His hands firmly grip my waist, my legs spread around his hips.

Jesus Christ.

"Preston, I…" My words are a stammering mess. "I-I didn't mean…" I swallow. "Whatever you think I am, I'm not, okay? Just please…" I bite my lip. "Please don't kill me or beat the shit out of me?" I plead.

Preston holds my gaze, a fire roaring behind his gray eyes.

"Red, I would never kill you. But if you want me to redden that pretty ass of yours, I'm up for the challenge."

My breath hitches at his words.

"Be sure of that, ok?" he breathes out, inching closer until the heat of his words brushes against my lips. "I'll start kissing you."

And then his lips are on mine, and the whole damn world flips upside down.

Damn it.

CHAPTER 4

Preston

The kiss awakens the beast inside me. Her lips taste like ripened raspberries, sweet and delicious.

I pull her closer, holding her tight like I never want to let her go. Fuck, I'm still unsure in what capacity she's working for the enemy.

But none of that matters. Not after that kiss. Hell, this girl could kill me with my own gun, and I'd still want to be kissing that sweet mouth. It's addictive.

It's feral and wild, and suddenly, it's like a dam comes crashing down. My hands slide into her fiery-colored hair, pulling it hard enough to make her gasp. I know damn well she can feel every thick inch of my rod against her sweet little cunt.

She wriggles those hips, and her hot little pussy soaks right through the denim of my jeans.

This girl was getting thoroughly fucked in her imagination. I know what I saw when I caught her in my bathroom, daydreaming. I know what I heard moaning from those pouty lips.

I wasn't feeding her lies before. I'm not the kind of guy she may have thought I was when I carried her like a fucking caveman into my cabin, and tossed her down on the couch. I'm also not the kind of guy who'd force a woman to do anything without consent, despite her obviously wanting it and being within arm's reach.

But a man can get to thinking all sorts of wicked thoughts, especially when he's got a little firecracker like London naked and on top of him.

When I think back to carrying her up the mountain and watching that skirt rise up her thighs, giving me just a peek of those cotton white panties, it was rough. Thinking of her in my tub was utter torture. I made sure not to touch her, but the second I left that room, I needed to touch something.

I made it past the threshold by a miracle, groaning as I sank against the doorframe fumbling with the zipper of my jeans. Then I wrapped my hand around my cock, groaning in pleasure. I grunted, stroking my thick shaft, watching the precum dripping down right to my balls.

I pictured her in my mind as I stroked faster. I wasn't touching her, and a part of me felt like being physically out of the room, even if it was just outside the door, made it okay.

I could hear soft mewling sounds coming from the en suite.

My cock swelled as my head swam. I couldn't hold back anymore. I was ready to explode.

Hearing my tempting little Red moan tipped me over the edge.

She softly rolls her hips once more, bringing me back to the moment. We're both driven by our animal instincts right now.

My mouth drops to her neck, my hands gripping her tightly as she moans. I kiss the sensitive skin there, biting her just enough to make sure she knows she's mine while digging my fingers into her hips. As my hands slide down over her soft curves, she starts to grind harder against the erection, tenting my jeans. She's so greedy, and I love it.

Her hands cup my jawline, and her mouth hungrily drops to my lips. I take control of the kiss with enough ferocity to bruise as my hands slide up over her hips and over every rib. When I sit up, she wraps her legs around my waist. I maneuver us so I can lift her from the floor, making her moan into my mouth as I walk us toward the bedroom and toss her onto my bed. Her pebbled little red nipples beg for my touch. When I pinch them, she cries out, causing me to groan in response.

In seconds, my t-shirt is off of my body and tossed onto the floor. Her eyes widen while ogling the wall of hard muscle and the short hairline under my navel. But all I see is her. Every gorgeous inch of her.

"Such a pretty pussy." Her eyes go wide, and her jaw drops as the heat blazes over her face. "You want my mouth on it, right?"

She bites her lips together and nods. Her pink core is open for my enjoyment. Right now, just for my eyes, soon enough, my mouth will be on it.

I'm salivating already. I drop to my knees in front of her, ready to give her another glimpse of the beast.

I bet no one's ever talked to her like that. I'm also betting no man has ever told her everything she wanted to hear. My little hellion likes dirty talking, more than that. She craves someone strong enough to ignite the fire hidden behind that innocent look.

"Just like this, little Red." My hands slide to her ass and cup it possessively, lifting her body the way I want it. A growl rumbles from my chest as I give her the first lap. She moans in delight.

Discovering what she likes turns me on, and my cock gets harder by the second. I'm consumed by a flame of pure need. *Need for her.* Just for her.

Another moan leaves her mouth, and her beautiful eyes are full of lust. My hands slide to her center, my fingers finding her tight channel, looking for the right spot to make her squirm.

London cries out as I hit the jackpot. My tongue pushes deep, greedy to get all her sweet honey, my groans rumbling through her tight body.

"Pinch your nipples for me, my little Red. Play with them while I'm feasting from your pussy."

I hear her low mewls… but that changes to cries of pleasure getting louder as her hips buck against me. My tongue slips up to swirl around her wetness, teasing her little nub and making her cry my name. One of her hands drops to my hair, tugging hard, holding me to her as I lick up every drop.

"Easy, love, I'm not going anywhere." There is no fucking way I'll leave this bed. I want more.

I make her squeal as I open her legs wider.

"God…" she moans, panting and writhing against my greedy mouth.

"This is what I do to trespassers" I drop a hand to undress. Yanking my belt away and tugging my zipper down. My jeans resting just beneath my ass. Her green eyes are wide as saucers as she watches me. My jeans slide over my hips, and my cock springs free, so fucking ready for action.

"Show me."

"I make them beg for my cock. Be a good little Red and make this pussy come over my fingers. Then if you're a good girl, I'll let you do it again around me."

I'm all alpha and, at this moment, definitely not a gentleman. London reaches her peak, and her whole body arches, almost levitating over the mattress, her pussy pulsating around my fingers. I continue my assault on her clit right through her climax as she presses her center against me, her nails clawing at my head, her honey dripping all over my tongue, the best thing I've ever tasted.

I've had a slice of her. I want more.

I want it all.

CHAPTER 5

Preston

I must be in paradise.

While tasting her sweetness as the last wave of her orgasm hits her, my tongue teases up and down her slit, licking up every drop of her cum. Fuck, she was made in heaven, but she's ready for sin.

I tear the rest of my clothes away from my body in two seconds, flat. I kiss and nibble her thigh before I slide up her body, her legs spreading wider. I'm going to make her all mine. First her pussy, then her little ass is next in line. I won't let a single inch of her go untouched.

Her body is my new playground.

She moans, wrapping her legs tight around my waist and kissing my mouth hungrily. She nips at my lip, stoking the fire inside of me.

"You're such a greedy little thing."

"You're an arrogant prick."

I ignore her sassy remark and continue to kiss her with no mercy.

Fuck, I want her so much. I need to be balls-deep in that tight little channel.

I want her to be aching because of me. I want her to be feeling me every time she moves. I want her to be missing my cock inside her.

I want to mark her. I want to claim her so that she never forgets.

I glance down, allowing my swollen tip to graze her pussy. Her soft, velvety pink folds part as I rub the head up against her.

I tease it over her nub, making her whimper as a drop drips on it, marking her with my cum.

It's the beast inside me wanting to spurt deep into her womb.

"Is this what you do?" London says between gasps for air.

"What? Teasing you? I told you I'd make you beg for my cock."

"Stop teasing me. Just fuck me already."

I kiss her, sliding my hand between us to align my cock at her entrance. Anticipating the feel of her wrapped around me.

A hard knock on the door bursts our bubble.

Who the fuck is here?

The wolf inside me roars.

The knocking continues, hard and fast. I'm not expecting anyone, and most know not to 'drop by' unannounced in these mountains. There are no scouts selling girl scout cookies around my land.

I turn to face London, this couldn't be good.

Regretfully, I pull away from her—my body already missing the feel of hers around me. I grab my jeans and shirt, throwing them on.

"London, don't move. And stay quiet."

I step out of the bedroom, close the double doors behind me, and walk toward my front porch. I snag the Colt I keep on the side table by the front door, slipping it into the back of my jeans. I glance out the side window, my eyes landing on the black pickup truck parked in my driveway.

One with the McCain Construction logo on the side of it.

Ladies and gentlemen, the shit show is about to start.

I know exactly what he's looking for here.

"Zachary," I greet him after I open the door. I eye the man standing on my front porch dressed in clean jeans and a checkered flannel shirt, his beard trimmed, and his hair combed back, giving the good boy vibe. This is all an act. Zachary isn't the sharpest pencil in the box. We all know that, starting with his uncle.

"Wolfe," he drawls and tries to peek inside my home.

Not happening on my watch, dipshit.

Zachary McCain is the nephew of Joseph McCain. Zachary runs one of the fronts for his family. A construction company that hasn't built a single shack around and has no workers on its payroll. We stare each other down, the two of us ready to duel. The tension running so thick in the air you could cut it with a knife.

Zachary is the muscle. He usually does his uncle's dirty work.

"What do you want, Zachary?" I demand. I don't give a fuck if he doesn't like my tone, or my words.

He eyes me, then spits over my porch's wooden floor.

"You should have more appreciation for your teeth. Do that again, and you will need extensive dental work," I warn him.

The bastard smirks.

"I'm looking for *something,*" he drawls. "I'm pretty sure it's here."

"Nothing of yours is on my property." I've claimed London. She's *mine* now. Just mine.

He just keeps smiling that creepy smile at me. "I really think it's around here."

I can't believe the balls on this man. At least he has the courage to come to face me. "What are you looking for, Zachary?"

I'm rewarded with an eye roll. Very mature for a grown-ass man.

"Red hair, nice rack. Cute ass, a mouth made for sin."

I want to rip out his teeth. I want to kick his ass off my porch. He just confirmed what I assumed. I know *who* he's after.

But I hold back, barely.

I need to be smarter than them. I need to figure out their plan.

"I can't help you. Go away," I say slowly.

Zachary's expression turns darker. "Don't try and fuck with me, Wolfe. We found her car near your property."

"In any case, why the fuck were you on my property?"

Zachary eyes me, and I'm so close to losing what little restraint I have. "Because I'm not stupid, Preston. I know how you take care of the security around here."

Zachary's scowl deepens, giving me a moment of pleasure.

"Give her to me, Wolfe!"

Never. But I manage to keep my face stoic.

"Who, Zachary?"

"You know who I'm talking about."

"I know that it's time for you to get the fuck off my property."

The fucker narrows his eyes, trying to look more dangerous. "You better watch yourself, Preston."

He turns, ready to spit on my porch again. But before he has the chance, I pull my Colt out, and he freezes. Slowly, he turns his head to stare at me.

"You're playing a dangerous game, Wolfe."

"I warned you."

Zachary eyes me, like he's contemplating doing it just to see if I'm bluffing. News flash, I'm not.

"Whatever," he says and shrugs.

He steps off the porch and walks to his truck, as if he has all the right to be here, in my driveway. He has no clue. I'm steps ahead of him. No one messes with a Wolfe and gets away with it.

"Just a last warning, Wolfe. Give me what I'm looking for, and I just might forget to tell my uncle that you pulled a gun on me." He warns before driving off, having the last word.

At least for now.

Vengeance is a dish best served cold, right?

CHAPTER 6

London

I found a blanket and wrapped it around my naked body. I needed some shield while waiting for him, while I watched from the window. The man, talking with Preston, is dressed like a lumberjack. If this were a famous fairytale, he would be here to rescue me.

This is utter madness. I'm still trying to figure out how I ended up here, captured by Mr. Big Bad Wolf, trapped in the mountains with him. Away from any help. Away from the world I've always known. Mind you, he is giving me the steamiest time of my life while dominating me, igniting a fire inside me like no one ever has.

And probably never will.

I couldn't hear much, but it's obvious they aren't on friendly terms. I also didn't miss how Preston pulled a gun on the man, which he is currently still holding as the man drives away.

A minute after that, the cabin's door closes behind Preston. Fury pours from him in waves. Maybe he believes I'm not a thief, but something shady is happening.

"Western Woods doesn't exist. You don't work there," he says quietly. His stare is full of menace. This is the version of wolf everyone around here is afraid of.

This again? Really? I explained to him already, why doesn't he believe me? I mean, call me an idiot, but I thought we ended that when we started tearing each other's clothes off. Plus, I'm not a good liar. He would have known if what I'm saying wasn't true.

"I'm not arguing with you again," I spat, turning away from him. "You know what? I should just call the garage for them to pick up my car and–..."

"There is no Western Woods." He continues as if I didn't say anything. "The company is a façade, London."

I turn and stare at him, disbelief all over my face. "I beg your pardon?"

"Do you have an office?"

My mouth falls open before replying: "Of course!" I'm not *an idiot.* The company that hired me is like every other in town.

"But it's not in a big building, right? You work in a remote office?"

I swallow with difficulty. *Yes.* That isn't uncommon these days.

"Mm-hmm… maybe." He's got me there, but I'm not admitting it that easily.

A smirk pulls his lips up. For a moment, I get distracted. Don't. I need to focus and fight harder.

"I'm right, aren't I, Red? How many coworkers have you met already?"

There aren't many. The company is just developing in this area. They told me they are hiring more staff shortly. For now, it's me, Webster, who comes in some days of the week, and Andrew. I think they sent him to Washington state, makes sense, right? There are a lot of trees there. That would be a great place to purchase more land.

"I've met several," I whisper. Fuck, fuck, fuck. I was so desperate to get a job I ended up messing with some shady ass people.

What the fuck.

"Am I right?"

I'm playing dumb. As if he couldn't read me as well as an open book. "What are you talking about?"

"Red, Western Woods is a façade. That's the reason I brought you here at gunpoint. I'm positive I know the people behind Western Woods, and who they really are. I'm starting to realize that you're not actually a part of that front."

I stare at him, my heart hammering hard inside my chest. "Part of… Part of what?"

What does he mean?

"There is no need to pretend, I saw you peeking through the window." He looks at me, arching a brow. "Connected to the fucker that just came here."

I give him a sheepish look.

"London, they're not good people. You're caught in the middle of something big. Something you obviously know nothing about."

I look at him dumbfounded, realizing how ignorant I've been.

"They hired you to do the dirty work."

"Please explain to me what you mean by dirty work."

"They're people with black souls, London. They must be using you as their scapegoat, knowing people wouldn't normally question someone like you—someone innocent."

"Who are they? Why are they so dangerous?"

"The McCains are a gang of cons. You can bet they've got their hands in everything shady around the county. Hard drugs, guns, illegal gambling, and prostitution. London, you have no idea the kind of shit they're into. How much blood they have on their hands." My hands tremble. Hearing the type of people I'm working for terrifies me. "They keep that stuff very well hidden, of course, behind a wall of fronts like Western

Woods. My guess is they're using WW to purchase a lot of land for below market value, the offer they sent you with is a shit. A land like this is worth millions, London. They are pretty rich, but they don't own that kind of money.

He has a point, and I'm starting to believe that something more is going on than a simple land deal.

Preston keeps talking: "Are they offering a big commission for the sale? I bet they aren't."

I shake my head, looking down and feeling like a stupid girl. They tricked me and without much effort. "Yeah, the money they offered isn't that much, but I need it, and quickly. My brother…"

"And if I'd said no, they'd have returned with eminent domain paperwork, signed off by some crooked politician in Sacramento and taken it from me anyway, yeah?"

"Yes." That's the ugly truth.

His chest vibrates with a growl, low and deep.

"What do you have that that fucker Zachary McCain wants?"

I give the matter some serious thought. "I have no idea. I've never met him before."

"Well, it must be something important for him to show up here unannounced. He knows I'm not the most welcoming host."

I bite my lip, almost not wanting to ask but knowing I can't stop the curiosity burning a hole in me. "Do you have your hands in it, too?"

His brows arch. "With the McCains?"

"No. All that stuff, the shady stuff." I whisper, afraid to ask. *Please say no, Preston, say no.*

"No. Absolutely not." Preston shakes his head. "My grandfather would whip my ass, he taught me better. I got my land, my business, and that's all I need."

His gaze racks over to me, so intense, telling me without any words that *that* isn't all he needs…

He wants me.

"But whatever Zachary's looking for, it's big. This is just the beginning, I'm sure."

"I have no idea what he's after. What the hell do they want with me? I'm not one of *his* girls, and I'll never be. That guy scared the hell out of me." If the man wants a piece of me, he needs to think again. I may be desperate for money, but not *that* kind of money.

"Did you take anything from WW?"

I shake my head. They never gave me a lot of information. "Other than the contract, I just have a USB with all the information about your land and some other properties around yours." I look around, searching for some answers.

"Are they really that dangerous, or are you telling me that because you despise the McCains?"

"They *are* that dangerous, London. They're not fucking around. This is heavy shit. They're fucking dangerous. And believe me, Red, they're not going to stop until they get what they want. Not just my land. They are looking for *you*."

I feel dizzy. My head is reeling. My entire body trembles while I hug the blanket around me. Suddenly, I'm chilled to the bone.

"I need to get back to LA. If I can get to my car and head back to the city, it's a big place. I'll blend in. I'll be safe there…"

He looks at me as if I've lost my mind.

"No. You're not going anywhere."

Preston's deep voice booms across the room, shaking me from my spiraling thoughts.

"You're staying here. Where I can protect you." He declares.

"No, no," I say, shaking my head. "If I vanish, I'm sure they'll eventually forget about me. I'm no one important, just a new agent."

"There's only one road heading off this mountain. They'll surely be posted at every corner around my property. And your car? I'm sure it's being tracked. They don't give two shits about trespassing."

He moves toward me with his eyes locked on mine.

"I won't let you go, London."

"You won't?" I ask in a low voice. "Because you can't, or because you don't want to?"

He keeps walking toward me. I don't realize I'm shaking until his big, strong hands slide beneath the blanket, and he grabs onto my hip.

"I can't, and I don't want to," he answers. "This mountain is the safest place for you. I can take care of you if you stay here with me."

Here with you? I won't be risking my life but upending it.

"You gonna stop me if I go?"

"Yes."

"And if I fight you? Try to run, anyway? Are you going to follow through and punish me by tying me to your bed?" I quirk my brow.

Preston pulls me against his hard chest, and I gasp at the almost animal-sounding growl that rumbles through his strong chest.

"Look at me," he whispers. "I'm thinking you might just like it if I do that. You want to be here. At my beck and call. Don't you, London? My little Red wants to be a bad girl."

I whimper in need. I can't even stop it, and I know damn well that he hears it.

"Say yes."

No man has ever touched me like him or spoken to me like this. I'm starting to believe no one in the entire world is like him.

Mr. Big Bad Wolf. The one and only Preston Wolfe.

He doesn't know the power he has over me, and I don't plan on telling him.

He tilts my face up to his. He cups my face and uses his other hand to grasp the nape of my neck, pulling me in to crush his lips to mine. The kiss is hard and deep until it feels like the whole world is spinning off its axis.

"You're staying here with me, London," he states, brooking no room for argument. "I'm not done with you—I'm not sure if I ever will be."

CHAPTER 7

Preston

I'm a man on a mission. I don't care about anything but her.

I growl, my rough, strong hands gripping her sweet body because it's mine to do whatever I want. Mine alone. I'm surprised none of the stuff on my breakfast bar hit the floor as we attacked each other. My mouth crushes to hers, sweet lips melting into me. London's naked after I yanked the blanket away and lifted her up. Her hands slip down my back and pull at my shirt, her fingers desperate to feel my skin.

Soon enough, she's going to feel every inch of me. Satisfaction guarantee.

I pull away just enough to tear my shirt completely off, and the next second, I'm crashing right back into her. Her nails rake down my back as my hand slides over her silky, bare skin. I'm a beast, my mouth traveling to her swan-like neck, my teeth marking her skin, getting lost in my passion.

With London's legs wrapped wide around my hips, I feel it when her fingers slip between us, down my abs to tug at my belt, making me growl like the wolf I am.

"My little Red knows who will eat her better, right?"

I nip at her shoulder, and she gasps sharply.

"Take it out and wrap those hands around me. I want you to feel how hard you make me, Red."

"This was your plan all along, wasn't it? You want to keep me here lusting after you?" she whispers with a mischievous spark in her green eyes. I groan as her fingers curl around my thick shaft, causing my cock to throb.

"You can try to run, Red. Just try me," I warn her. "You can bet your sweet ass that I will catch you. And when I do…"

A tremor of excitement makes her body shiver.

"Oh… fuck… Preston."

Not yet, but soon.

"Imagine my hand reddening that little ass of yours, Red." She says nothing, but I can read her reaction. Excitement. Curiosity. Eagerness. "You like that, don't you? You may act like you're a good, proper girl, but I can see you like it dirty. Don't try to deny it." I think I've found my perfect match. She may act like a lady on the streets, but she'll be a slut in my sheets.

"Harder, London. Fuck me with your hands as hard as I'll fuck your little pussy."

London moans, her hands stroking me faster as her head drops back. She's enjoying this as much as I am.

I nibble her neck again as I slide one hand between us, teasing it down her flat abdomen until the pads of my fingers roll over her clit.

"You won't want to run away once I'm done with you, Red. You won't be able to walk straight for a week."

My finger rolls in slow circles over her little button, keeping her gasping and whimpering, dripping her sweet honey all over my fingers. I move her hand so I can ease forward, and when the thick, swollen head of my cock teases against her entrance, it takes all my self-control to not plunge right in.

"You're gonna come so hard you'll see stars. But only when I say you can."

I pin her to the counter as I drive my cock inside her body.

"You make me feel so good," London says after catching her breath. Her hands can't stop clawing at my back while her legs tighten around me like she's trying to pull me in even deeper. "You, Mr. Big Bad Wolf, are bad, which is very, very good."

Her sassy little comment makes me chuckle. "Just for you. Now, be a good little Red and take every inch of me," I growl through my gritted teeth.

She said I make her feel good. But she has no idea how she makes *me* feel. Like the goddamn alpha of the pack.

Her eager pussy contracts all around me, like she's trying to milk me. Who am I to deny her?

"That's it, Red," I grit out, pushing another inch inside. "Now open up and let me in."

I tighten my hold on her ass and piston the rest of my swollen cock deep inside her warm pussy.

A scream of pleasure escapes her. "You… Mr. Wolfe… have an extremely… big cock." London declares breathlessly.

"The better to fuck you with," I reply with wickedness in my tone. Looking down at the sight of her on my shaft is making me dizzy with arousal.

She's drenching my rigid length.

Dripping all over my dick. I love how greedy she is for it. It's like she's wordlessly begging for more.

"You can't get enough of my cock inside you, can you, my little Red?"

London gasps for air as I pound into her harder.

"Tell me, London, what do you want? Use your words, not just your body."

"Yes! Give it to me!" she cries in rapture. "Give me what's mine."

I'm eager to give her whatever she needs… she just called me hers… my hips move faster.

I grin. She has no idea how sexy she is when she knows what she wants and isn't afraid to ask for it.

I roll my hips and drive my cock deeper inside her. We both groan in pleasure. Red begins to blur my vision.

She's mine to possess.

She's mine to claim.

She's. All. Mine.

With that final thought, I unleash the beast and fuck her like an animal.

I can feel her body trembling against mine, her thighs clenching around me. With each of my dominating thrusts, my jeans finally drop to the floor. We're both so hot for each other. She's the air to my flame, ready to burn like a back draft. Together we're explosive.

Thinking of her staying here makes me wild. London here with me every day, sharing my home, my time, everything. Sounds amazing.

Her need for me shows in the marks she makes across my back, and I can feel that sweet little cunt tightening up. She's about to reach the peak of this mountain.

"Preston!" My name on her lips sounds so good.

"You want to come all over the Big Bad Wolf's cock, Red? You want to feel me deeper than any other man has ever been before. I want to feel you come. I want to feel you drenching my cock. When you come, know that you're mine. All mine. Come for me, London. Now."

I rock my hips forward, hitting her cervix. Driving in so deep that she can feel me in her womb.

She cries out as her entire body arches against me as her orgasm spreads over her like a wildfire. I'm tempted to follow her over the edge, but I somehow hang on.

I pull out of her and scoop her into my arms while I turn toward the kitchen table.

I'm not done with her yet.

I place her down in front of the table and bend her over. I caress up and down her back.

"You didn't come. Don't you want me?" she whispers while looking at me over her shoulder... I slide my hand up into her hair, tugging it into my fist. After I pull her up, our lips crash together and she melts into my hold.

"I want you in every way I can get you, London," I murmur heatedly. My cock is rock-hard throbbing against her ass.

I lower myself into the chair, slowly guiding her down onto me.

"Just like this," I growl, encouraging her. My muscles are tight as London lowers down. My blood roars like fire in my veins as I watch her small body slowly take every inch of me.

She's torturing me with every roll of her hips. Well, I'll happily do the same to her, for hours.

Her body, welcoming mine, is a magnificent view.

It's like we're finding this need in each other, that we never knew was missing. One-night stands could never compare to this. I squeeze her ass as she rides me, spreading her cheeks. The puckered hole at her rear entrance is tempting me. I tease it. One day I will claim this hole too.

"Oh God…" London gasps, panting as she slowly gets used to the feel of me from this angle. "Preston!"

Good thing I don't have any neighbors. She's allowed to scream my name as much as she wants. She reaches out an arm, gripping the edge of the table. Slowly rising and falling, it's better than any lap dance I've ever had.

Her thighs start to quiver when she eases off me until just the crown remains inside.

"Ride me, Red," I demand, my hands tight on her ass, gripping her.

My fingers leave marks on her skin and fuck if that doesn't fuel the beast inside me.

"I want to watch you bounce on my dick again and again. You want to tame the animal, little Red?"

"Make me yours."

"Tame the beast," I growl, my heavy balls twitching. "Ride your wolf, take what you want. Until you come all over it like the good little Red you are."

My hand smacks down against her ass, making her cry with pleasure, her back arching as she starts to ride me harder and faster. My hands go to her perky tits, tweaking her hard nipples.

The hot, wet, erotic sounds of skin against skin are driving me crazy. I spank her again, feeling her pussy clench. Her glistening cream drips down my shaft, and my balls start to tighten as I pass the point of no return.

"Keep fucking my cock like that, Red. You're gonna make me come so hard for you."

"Yes, please."

"I'm going to give you every single drop that you'll be so full of me. Ride your beast, Red. Now fucking come for me."

And she complies. Beautifully.

London shudders in pleasure as her hot little pussy clamps down around me, and her body ripples with her climax. She throws her head back, melting back into me as my arms go around her body, pulling her tight as I thrust deep inside and let go. It's like a bomb going off. I roar into her skin, holding her to the base of my cock as I explode into her.

I kiss down the back of her neck as she pants for air.

I'll keep her safe, and while I do, I'm going to keep her full of me. One day, I want her swollen with our child.

She's mine now. And I protect what's mine.

CHAPTER 8

London

I'm exhausted. But my body is thrumming with excitement.

I'm panting as I fall back onto his mattress, my body still sweaty and tingling from the little scene we just had in the kitchen. I almost passed out after coming so hard. It's not just his cock—although it's impressive—but it's his hands, and his mouth, and the things he says to me. I've never been handled this way. He's said multiple times that I'm his, but what does that mean? I'm too afraid to ask, if I must be honest.

But talking about the good stuff… How many orgasms can one woman have before her heart stops?

I'm really curious if it's possible to pass out from coming. With him though? Yeah, I'm willing to investigate more. Just for research purposes, of course.

Preston comes into the bedroom with a steaming cup of coffee in his hand, gloriously naked. Even at rest, his dick is impressive, and my mind is reeling with the need to play with it. I've been so distracted by the things he does *to* me that I haven't had a chance to get a taste.

He's perfect, sculpted muscles that tighten as he pads toward me like he's a beast stalking its prey. And, of course, that's what I am—his prey.

Preston Wolfe is an animal in all the ways that count.

I lick my lips, salivating at the view of his rippling abs to the deep grooves of his muscles that point like an arrow down to his dick.

Preston is huge. I mean, the girth alone is impressive, and don't even get me started on his length. So smooth and perfect, his crown a darker shade, with a single thick vein running down the length of it. I swallow, squeezing my thighs together as I stare unabashedly.

"Do you like what you see?"

"Yes."

Preston smirks that roguish smile that makes my pulse race. "You're looking at my dick like you want a taste."

I bite my lip. "Uh… maybe."

He chuckles, moving closer. "Cat got your tongue?"

"You said I'm staying—" I mumble as he cuts me off.

"Don't even think about leaving? I'll tie you to that bed if you even try." The spark in his eyes tells me he would be more than happy to do it.

"You want me to try to leave, don't you?"

I shiver, and he notices.

"Get on your knees, London," he demands, prowling toward the side of the bed.

I do as I'm told and get on my knees, taking a good look at his big cock. It's getting thicker, until his full erection is bobbing in my face. I gulp as I imagine taking him into my mouth. He wraps his hand around it. It is so sexy, but I want to be the one to do that. I want that to be my hand. My fingers sliding all over him.

And then I want my mouth wrapped around him. Licking him with my tongue.

His fingers brush my jaw, and I shiver as he tilts my chin up so that his eyes lock with mine.

"London, open your mouth," he whispers. His gravelly tone is deep.

He's whispering, but his words are clearly a direct order. There's a demanding roughness to it that has me drowning with lust.

"You like being ordered around. You want to give up control."

"I-I…"

I stammer as his hand slides into my hair, fisting the red strands and tugging just enough to make my scalp hurt. I love it.

"I'm sure you have never let anyone dominate you the way I do. The way you like it. Never before have you been open enough to allow a man to fuck you like you've always wanted. You want—and you need—a man who takes control and makes you his."

Never. Ever. Just with him. I don't know why, but I feel it in my bones. I can trust Preston Wolfe.

His filthy words burn through my body, turning me on.

"Tell me if I'm wrong, Red."

"You're right," I reply. *So fucking right.*

"I'm fucking your face. Open your mouth and take me deep, my good little Red."

He pulls me against him. There's a roughness to him, but it's just the right amount.

I've never wanted to submit before and let go completely.

I don't know what it is, his arrogance or cockiness. Or maybe it's just that Preston is a special brand of man. A captivating, gorgeous man, who's rough, yet tender—the alpha of the pack.

He looks down at me, daring me to defy him. But I don't. I open my mouth as he thrusts hard right to my throat, making me gag.

An animalistic growl escapes him.

My lips stretch around him, trying to take all of him. Preston's hand tightens in my hair, sending a thrill through me as I swipe my tongue across his swollen head. He pulls me off him.

"Get on the bed. On your hands and knees."

I quickly obey.

There's no hesitation when he begins to fuck my face like he was fucking my pussy, with unrestrained power. I can feel him feeding me with his length. Fire explodes through me. I'm so lost in him that I'm barely aware that I'm reaching down between my legs.

"That's it, touch yourself for me. Play with your pussy. Get it ready. Make it nice and wet." Those are my fingers, but I'm following his command.

I moan wildly, the vibrations traveling through his cock. My lips slide up and down his swollen shaft. He leans over me, one of his big hands gliding down my back until he cups the cheeks of my ass. One of his long fingers searches between my legs until he finds what he's looking for. His fingers join mine as I roll my clit, and when he starts to ease two of them inside my pussy, my entire body is burning, and he's peppering the flames with gunpowder.

Preston grunts deeply, his fingers plunging in and out of me, making me even wetter. While I tease my clit over and over again. His cock throbs between my lips, and when his hand tightens in my hair, the need brewing inside me makes me crazy.

Suddenly, he rolls me over as his cock bobs above my face. I lean up, and when my tongue swirls tentatively over his heavy balls, he growls in pleasure.

"That's it. Suck me deep. Your mouth on me feels so good, baby," he hisses. I moan around them, slurping and swirling my tongue over them.

His muscled body coils as he spreads my legs wide. His hands slide over me, teasing between my legs. One hand plays with my aching clit, as the other curls two fingers deep inside. I moan wildly at his touch.

My orgasm is about to crash over me as his amazing fingers take control.

"You're about to come, aren't you? I want you to hold it and come with me," he growls. "Now be a good little Red and make me come. I'm going to come all over you."

His thumb moves with practiced strokes. I moan louder while swirling my tongue over him as I clutch his sac with one hand while stroking his cock with the other. His balls tighten, the volcano ready to erupt. His cock throbs while Preston roars and explodes. There is no other word to describe it. He comes hard, which sets me off. We both come hard—together.

He pulls away, and I think he's about to lay with me on the bed, but suddenly, he's moving between my legs. I gasp as he yanks my legs up over his muscled forearms and eases into me.

"You're still hard?"

He grunts while he leans down until our torsos are pressed together. "You've cast a spell over me, Red. I'm always hard when you're around." Then his mouth is on mine, kissing me deeply. Preston Wolfe is my alpha, and I want to follow him forever.

"Now I'm gonna fuck you harder. I want to keep you here, in my bed, wrinkling up my sheets. The moment I caught you in my trap, I knew I wanted to keep you."

He fucks me with abandon, voiding my mind of any rational thought. I know he's saying the right things, but I can't focus on them. I cry out each time he bottoms out.

It feels dirty, hotter than hell, wicked as sin, and it's the sluttiest I've ever felt.

And I can't get enough.

There is no mountain, no danger looming over us. No war between the Wolfes and the McCains.

Nothing else matters outside our bubble.

Our bodies collide again and again until suddenly, everything crashes around us. It's a supernova. I cry out at my orgasm as he continues to drive even deeper, and when he comes, I can feel him filling me up. Leaving me floating into the void. I feel weightless.

"I'm never gonna let you go, London. Never."

What is he saying? I move my head, opening my eyes slowly and locking my gaze with his.

"Okay." Is my reply, unsure of how the hell to tell the man I just met that I never want to leave him, that I just want to stay here—where I feel comfortable, safe, and cherished—without sounding like a lunatic.

I don't care if someone tells me I'm nuts. His brand of crazy feels pretty good.

CHAPTER 9

Preston

I'm in big trouble.

This girl came from out of nowhere, rocking my world. She's turned my life upside down—and as crazy as it sounds—it feels right.

Maybe I should ask myself *what the fuck* is happening? I'm falling in love with her. There is no way—or reason—to deny it. Facts are facts.

I'm not the right guy for her, but fuck if I'm gonna let her go. I'm falling—hard and fast—it's making my head spin. I met her hours ago, and at the same time, it feels like I've known her forever.

What do I know about being in love? Nothing. My only relationships have been with my cousins and my grandfather. But never with a woman. They never last more than a couple of drinks and a quick fuck.

I've been too busy. There's always been too much to do with taking over the mountain, trying to do right by my grandpa, and staying out of trouble. Here, the only rule is survival of the fittest. The wolf that shall break it must die, as an old poem says. And this old wolf isn't ready to check out of this world.

Not when I just found her.

I thought all I wanted was this mountain and a life of my own. I got the mountain, and I believed I was living my best life until the moment she fell right into my arms.

This woman. A chance at starting my own family.

Fuck, I've lost my freaking mind. We barely know each other, but I know myself enough to admit to what I feel. This isn't just sex. The chemistry between us is as unexpected as an avalanche. There was something mind-blowing and messy about the idea of coming inside of her with nothing between us and creating something new and exciting together. It wasn't just some crazy fantasy.

With her, it's all I want.

She's way more than a random fling. Because a fling means that this is temporary, and there is nothing temporary about this. She can't leave, not with this bond growing and intensifying between us. I want her to stay.

Fucking hell, I need her to stay.

I know I'll come off like I'm crazy by asking her, but it's all I want.

How do I ask a woman like her to stay, be my wife, and have my kids?

We're up on the patio, enjoying the warmth of the fire while sipping hot cocoa. I brought her out here because it's one of my favorite spots, perfect for gazing at the stars.

We've talked about a lot of things. She told me about her brother and how she's providing for him, which is why she started working for Western Woods.

She doesn't need to worry about it anymore. From this moment on, I'll take care of everything.

I tell her about my military past. My two cousins, who are like my brothers. My grandfather. How much this land means to me.

"You think your brother would like it here?"

"I think he'd love it," she replies. But suddenly, her expression morphs. A sadness shadowing her pretty face.

"He can stay here with us for as long as he wants," I state. This is her home too. The sooner she realizes that, the better. "We'll bring him here as soon as possible."

"You want to bring my brother here?"

"Of course."

She says nothing, but I can feel the tension leaving her body. She wants to stay as much as I want her to. A man knows when he's found *the one.* That's what she means to me. She's my one.

"This is heavenly," she whispers after a while of comfortable silence. Her mouth trails a path over the strong line of my jaw. Her sweet lips feel warm. The beast in me is idle, but never too far away.

"Careful, little Red, keep doing that, and you'll wake the beast. Behave like the good girl you say you are."

London sighs. "I *am* always a very good girl. Never broke my curfew, straight A's. After college, I went to get my MBA."

"With all those accreditations, how did you end up working for a shitty company like Western Woods?"

"There was another job offer, but…" She sighs, shaking her head. "Desperation. With my brother's bills coming every month and my savings dwindling, I couldn't wait for a month or two for the normal hiring process. WW was looking for a quick start and well…"

After hearing her explanation, I want to kill that fucker McCain even more.

"Plus, after…"

"After what?" I ask, feeling her body tense between my arms.

"We're having a good time," she murmurs. "Let's not talk about it."

"I want to know," I growl. "Hell, London, I want to know every damn thing about you. Everything."

She tells me about her dumbass of an ex. I sit and listen until she's done, even though my blood pressure is going through the fucking roof, and all I want to do is go to LA, find this fucker, and kill him.

"So, that's it," she sighs.

I shake my head, pulling her close again. "If I ever see him, I'll knock his fucking teeth out."

She giggles, leaning up to kiss me slowly and then deeper.

"Or maybe I should buy him a drink."

She scowls, her eyes just a slit. "For?"

"He was an idiot, he lost you, and now you're here with me."

"Wow. You're good." A beautiful smile draws on her lips. Incapable of resisting, I steal another kiss.

"I'll show you good."

"Wha—" she starts to say, but I silence her with my mouth.

We start to tear off the layers of fabric between us. She's bare before me as she straddles my hips. As my lips close around a red hard nipple, she moans. I swirl my tongue around it, making it pucker in my mouth. My hands slide down her back, moving over the soft curve of her perfect round ass and holding her tight.

She grinds herself against me. I can feel her slick cunt dripping all over my cock, and when I move my mouth to her other nipple, she only grinds down harder.

I grip her ass and lift her up, nudging the throbbing crown against her opening. She trembles, and I grit my teeth.

She slides down every thick inch of me until I can feel her clit rubbing against my pelvis. I growl, as she starts to ride me, taking whatever she wants from me.

"Ride me, little Red," I groan. "Let me feel that pretty pussy."

So she does.

"I can feel that this sweet little pussy has never been stretched like this. Your pussy is made to fit my cock, and only mine. No other dick will compare, and you'll never get a chance to find out. Now, ride me and show me who this sweet cunt belongs to."

"Oh, God!" London cries out, clinging to me, her thighs tightening around me as she starts to buck even faster. "I love your big cock. I never want to stop fucking this thick, perfect… fuck!"

She screams, biting my shoulder as she comes, her pussy clamping down on my shaft and rippling along my length. I groan, grabbing her ass and riding her through her orgasm. My fingers trace her skin as she gasps for air, moaning and kissing me deeply as she trembles in her aftershocks.

I thrust up, making her whimper as my cock fills her to the hilt.

"Ready for more?"

"I don't ever want to stop."

I grin, hungrily kissing her as I tease her tight little pucker.

"I think you like that, don't you?" I growl as she nods, giving me the green light.

"Yes," she moans.

"You want me to claim every hole, don't you?"

She gasps, clenching for a second before she melts into me. I ease a finger inside her tight little ass, stretching and preparing her for me.

"My little Red, such a dirty girl." Fuck, I could come just from listening to the sounds she makes.

"Fuck, London…"

"Preston, I-I want you to…"

"To what? Fuck your ass?"

She replies by reaching back and between us, her fingers teasing my balls before they circle around my cock. She strokes me with the head still inside her pussy, making me groan and grit my teeth. Slowly, she eases off me, and when she slips my cock back, I move my finger aside. London gasps quietly as she centers my cock against her tight, forbidden asshole, her eyes widen as she chews on her lip.

"I can't even explain it," she whispers. "But you're all I want, and I'm all yours. You said I wouldn't or couldn't run because I was yours?"

I nod, our eyes locked and my heart racing.

"Well, I am," she says quietly. "I'm all yours."

"Stay," I growl. Fuck it, it just comes out, and I don't care. "Stay and spend forever with me. I promise I'll do everything for you to be my queen. I'll fuck you exactly how you deserve to get fucked, the way you like it. This mountain, the house, everything I have is yours, London. Just say you'll stay…"

CHAPTER 10

London

"This could all be yours, with me."

"Preston," I moan as he kisses me softly.

"London…"

Why wouldn't I want to stay? He's my dream man and everything I could ever want.

I'm lost in him. Deliciously, wonderfully, hopelessly lost. I might be crazy, but I know without a doubt that this is real. Being here with him feels like home.

Not over twenty-four hours have passed since we crossed paths, but I've already connected with Preston on a level I've never felt with anyone.

I can't ignore it.

I can't deny it.

I kiss him as I feel him start to fight against my ring of muscles. I groan into his lips, feeling the tip of that huge, throbbing dick push against that forbidden place. It's so fucking dirty and so hot. So good, like nothing I've ever imagined before, and I just want more.

Holy fuck.

"Just like that, little Red," he groans into my ear. "Take every inch of me. Feel me deep, claiming you, and taking what no man has ever taken. Tell me if I'm hurting you, and I'll stop."

"Fuck me, fuck me, fuck me!" I scream at the pressure of his thrusts.

"Take that cock, my dirty little Red. I want to feel you grip me so tight when you come. I want you to know what it feels like to come so fucking hard with my big dick deep in your sexy little asshole. Take that big cock, Red, and come for me."

For a second, I almost think I've blacked out. Suddenly, everything explodes. I scream, the orgasm detonating through me like a fire peppered with TNT and my body shattering under the force of it.

I feel him coming inside my most forbidden place while his roars of pleasure mix with mine, and I climax once more.

His fingers brush a strand of sweaty hair from my face, and when his lips brush my ear, I grin and sink against him.

"That was…" I have no words to describe it.

"It was what?" Preston whispers into my ear.

"Out of this world," I exclaim, turning to face him as our lips fuse together.

We're stretched out next to each other on the blanket, looking up at the stars. The cold doesn't bother me. I can't stop grinning as the heat of Preston's body keeps me all cozy and warm.

I snuggle against him. There's nothing sexual about it, just a loving, tender caress I will cherish forever.

Being here with him seems to have put my life in perspective.

I've never felt this uninhibited with anyone. Being here gives me this sense of freedom I've never known before. I'm unsure if it's the fresh air and the stars, or the mystery surrounding a man like him, but either way, I'm content.

"I want to stay here with you," I whisper softly while kissing him. Preston arches a brow, and my heart skips a beat.

Did he say all those things just because we were fucking?

No, I don't think so. We were talking about bringing my brother here. He said this is my home too. He's called me his. Several times.

And if I'm his, he's mine too. Completely and unabashedly. Without boundaries or regrets. Preston Wolfe is mine.

"You asked me earlier to stay here."

Our eyes lock, and something sparks in his steely eyes. He understands what I mean.

I gasp as he scoops me into his arms and kisses me deeply.

I'm so lost in him that the noise is just that. Background noise. My brain doesn't register the danger at first. I feel so safe here, so freaking happy. It's not until Preston roars and shoves me down. He covers me with his body as something explodes near us. I start to scream bloody murder.

CHAPTER 11

Preston

What. The. Fuck.

She's safe in my arms. Thank God.

I know London's scared out of her mind, and every part of me hates to let go of her, but I need to assess the damage. I must know who just emptied a whole fucking clip into the side of my home.

Fucking McCains. How dare they have the balls to come and attack me in my territory?

They are playing with fire.

The war has begun.

Bring it on, motherfuckers.

"Stay here and stay down," I instruct her, kissing her lips before standing and running for the back door. Maybe the bastards are leaving already, but they won't get away that easy. My years in the Army have prepared me. I grab my cell phone from the kitchen counter to activate the sequence for my traps on my property. Then I grab my Colt from the drawer.

My cabin is a mess. Splintered wood, broken windows, smoke, and water is pouring from the sprinkler system, covering everything in the living room and putting out the fires. With my gun in hand, I walk to one of the side windows as a truck door slams shut and tires kick up gravel as the vehicle roars down the driveway. They haven't gotten far when the motion-activated explosives detonate. Gotcha, asshole. Someone shouts, causing a deep level of satisfaction to roll over me.

The pitch-black night is only lit by the flames coming from the porch. I run to grab a couple of extinguishers to put them out.

While I fight to douse the flames, I check out the extent of the damage—the porch is beyond repair, but the cabin is in good shape. The steel I used to build the place, along with the thick treated logs, made the building strong and stable. Where is the card that ATF agent gave me months ago? With my blood pumping and my muscles clenched, I search my phone for the video recording. Three fuckers, bathing my porch with gasoline, all have their faces covered, but from another angle, the plate of the vehicle is visible, as is the logo on the tailgate.

Shit. I know that truck.

Fucking Zachary McCain.

The card I'm looking for should be in my desk.

I'm still seeing red when a soft hand slides around my torso and fingers settle over my hard abs. The movement startles me, but the softness of her skin calms me instantly. She's here with me, blinking as I turn to find London sliding behind me, still wrapped in the blanket. She slips her arms around me.

"You were supposed to stay where I told you," I grumble.

"And you're not supposed to blow up half the mountain," she bites back, glaring at me. "What happened?"

The sharp look in her eyes makes me grin. She may be scared, but her strength shows through.

"I had to deliver a message."

"And?"

"Zachary McCain was here. The fucker knows you're here, and he wants you back."

Her pretty lips open in shock. "He what?"

I give her a glare. "I told you, these people are dangerous, London. And they want you back for business. You mean money to them, in one way or another. We need to find out why. The faster, the better."

"I…" She blinks in confusion. A grim expression crosses her face before I circle my arms around her. *I'm here to protect you, Red,* I want to say with every cell of my body.

I'm here. You're safe with me. I'd die for you.

"I don't want anything to do with them," she says fiercely. "I'm staying here with you."

"They're going to come back, London. And when they do—and I'm saying when, not if—they come looking for you again, we're going to be ready for them."

I close my eyes for a moment and replay the video again in my head. My imagination is running wild. What if London gets hurt?

I've tried to stay out of all the drama since I came back here. Live and let die, that's my motto. Joseph McCain knows that, and he's always respected that. I never shit on his turf, and he never came and shit on my mountain.

What happened? I have the thought that Zachary is acting weirder than usual, and London is at the eye of the tornado.

My jaw clenches in determination, the pure rage at what could almost have happened building up inside of me. She could have been hurt or worse. I just fucking found her, after pretty much accepting that I'd never find that one woman who could make me feel this way.

I've kept the peace for a long time. But it seems like staying out of this mess isn't working any longer.

Lines have been crossed. They've come after what's mine and put what's mine in harm's way.

"Are you okay?" I whisper, burying my face in her silky red hair. She nods.

"Perfectly," she replies. "You?"

"Well enough."

London just looks at me, heat sparkling in those green eyes I've come to love. "You're still naked."

I chuckle. I'm ready to show her the truth of my feelings. Actions are better than words. But my fucking phone starts to ring.

I bet that's one of my cousins, they should hear the alarm.

"Damian," I greet him and then start the briefing.

"Fuck, bro. This is deep shit. What do you want me to do? Are you sure Zachary is on this?"

I have video evidence, and I'm sure if I walk a couple of hundred yards, his truck will be on my driveway. "One hundred percent."

"Fuck." Damian swears. "Are you sure this girl isn't working for them?"

London was just a pawn in this intricate chess game, I'm sure of it.

She's sitting on the couch with her laptop while furiously typing. If I had to guess, she's looking for information on the USB Western Woods gave her. There are pieces of this fucked-up puzzle scattered everywhere. She's put on a pair of my joggers and a sweatshirt. The clothing isn't her size, and yet somehow, she still looks gorgeous wearing them.

I nod. "Yeah, I know so. Do you know anything about this fake wood trading company's connection with Zachary's construction company?"

There is a muted conversation between them. I'm sure they are on their way here.

"Nothing we know about. Maybe Zachary is drumming up his own business just outside of McCain's reach."

Interesting. That could be a viable option.

"There's word that Zachary is smuggling drugs over the border."

Shit. I never thought he'd go behind his uncle's back.

"If I'm going after Zachary, I need more information. Something undeniable," I muse out loud, scratching my chin. As the lawyers say, beyond a reasonable doubt.

"Coming over, bro," he says. "Julian is dealing with a stubborn client. But I'm ready to help."

I frown. "There is no need. You run a business…"

"Preston…"

"Yeah."

"We are family, Preston. I'm on my way."

I groan. Yeah, this is what family is all about. "Okay, bro, see you in a while."

"You betcha." He clears his throat. "So, this new chick…"

"Careful," I warn him. "You're talking about my woman…"

I hear my cousin chuckling. *The fucker…*

My eyes move across the room, just taking her in.

A smile pulls my lips up.

"She worth the possibility of going to war with the fucking McCains?"

"I'd go to war with the whole world for her." I declare with no hesitation.

"That's good to know," Damian growls.

After that, I call my grandpa. The sooner he knows about this, the better. This is worse than being briefed by my CO in the Army. My grandpa lives in Rosarito, about an hour south of the border, but he has eyes and ears everywhere.

"I've got Damian coming over."

My grandfather groans. "Fuck, Preston. Are you planning to make a mess? You know how impulsive your cousin can be."

I scowl. I know he's right, but it's the only option I've got. I can't do this alone. "Yes, I'm sure."

"Good luck, son," my grandpa rumbles into the phone. "You're gonna need it."

He pauses.

"And after this shit ends, bring that girl here," he says. "I want to meet the woman who stole my boy's heart."

CHAPTER 12

London

I sip more coffee and keep searching through the folders in the USB WW provided me. This is insane. It's like looking for a needle in a haystack. Mostly because I'm not sure what I'm looking for.

The tension is heavy here, and there's that little fact that we have people who want us dead. That's something I can't ignore.

I look up. Preston is in the kitchen, casually making tomato soup and grilled cheese sandwiches. Even with some crazy mountain psychopaths after us, all of this just feels, well, perfect.

Looking at Preston, even now, with the threat looming over us, I can't help but feel the heat tease through me. God help me. I want him again. I want him to march right over here and tear our clothes off.

I force myself to focus on the Western Woods data. Zachary wants something here, even if I can't for the life of me figure out what it is. In another folder, is a contract for trying to buy Preston's land, and another for one of his cousins, who lives a couple of miles away. There are also a few maps of mountains that highlight some of the old railroads running through it, but that's all.

As a pair of headlights shine through the broken front windows, Preston's mood changes, and he jumps into action. He runs to the front door. The cannon of his gun, ready to put a bullet between the eyes of the intruder.

"I need you to stay down," he growls. I nod as I slip to the floor right by the couch, my heart racing. The sound of a truck engine turns off. Then, silence follows.

Preston's jaw tightens, and his finger slips over the gun's trigger as he peers out the side window into the dark driveway. Suddenly, the door to the kitchen opens. I gasp, and Preston roars as he turns to point his gun at the intruder.

A dark figure steps in.

"You are crazier than I thought," Preston says while shaking his head and putting his gun down.

Preston's shoulders ease as he jabs a finger at the man. The guy is as tall and built as Preston, but with dark hair to Preston's almost black and eyes that glint full of mischief. He smiles at Preston.

"Just keeping you on your toes, bro."

I exhale, slowly getting off the floor. This is Preston's cousin, Damian.

"I could have blown your brains out," Preston growls

"In your dreams. I'm quicker than you."

Damian grins. He's in black jeans, military boots, and a gray Henley. His eyes dart past his cousin, locking on me and making me shiver just a little bit. Why are all the family men this intense?

Damian comes and greets Preston with a pat on the shoulder, and then his attention is on me.

"Hello there," he purrs, the corners of his lips curling along that perfect jaw. He pushes past his cousin and steps toward me. "I don't think we've become acquaintances yet, gorgeous. I'm…"

Preston's hand shoots out, closing hard on Damian's arm, shoving him away from me.

"Fuck off, Damian."

Damian grins. "Just testing the waters, man." He turns his attention to me. "Sorry, just making sure this asshole was for real about the way he just babbled about you on the phone."

Preston scowls before protesting loudly. "I didn't babble."

"He totally did." Preston's cousin says with a theatrical eye roll.

I grin as Preston's gaze meets mine. He winks while letting go of his cousin's arms. "Just watch yourself," he warns Damian.

"Where are your manners, motherfucker? Offer me a drink."

"Talking about manners." Preston scowls. "You understand the issue we are about to face, right? I'm sure a battalion of McCain's men is heading here."

"That's the reason I need a fucking drink."

I chuckle as Preston shakes his head. "Help yourself. I'm not your maid."

Damian grins, roguish and cocky. "You're not my type of maid anyway."

This time Preston is the one rolling his eyes. "Thanks for coming."

"I've checked the perimeter. Everything is in place." Damian grins, and I wonder what that means. Bombs? Traps?

"Anyway, I'd never turned down the chance to shoot some McCains?" Damian continues, taking a big pull of his whiskey. Then his blue glance is on me. "You're caught up in this because they sent you to deal with my cousin here and make him sell the land?"

A resigned sigh escapes from my lips. The situation is insane. "Yes," I admit. "I live in LA. I didn't know how things work around here. They tricked me."

Damian grins. "You get a pass. We all know how they are here, so we can smell McCain bullshit a mile away."

"Did you find anything?" Preston asks. I shake my head, stepping into his hold.

"Nothing yet."

Preston takes my face between his hands, tilting my face up with a finger under my chin, then whispers, "I'm not gonna let anything happen to you."

He kisses me slowly and softly, and I melt into him.

"Awwww, you guys are so cute. I hate to burst your little bubble, lovey-doveys. We need to focus," Damian clears his throat. "They are here."

He nods at a few trucks coming up the driveway. Preston growls, grabbing his gun and then a shotgun from under the kitchen counter, and Damian even loses the smile as he pulls out two guns from the waist of his jeans.

"This time, listen to me and go and stay in the room," Preston says. "Take the laptop and all your stuff there. Don't come out until I go and look for you."

"No, Preston, I want to stay with you. You promised…"

"London," he says quietly. My name on his lips is like a spell, as is his hand sliding around my waist, holding me against his hard chest. "I promised to keep you safe. That's what I'm doing. If things go out of control, I want you to look for the hidden room behind the carpet in front of the bed. I need to deal with these bastards. I can't do that if I don't know you're safe."

Safe room? Things out of control? This is worse than I thought.

"And right by your side is the safest place to be." I protest. "You're my heart, Preston. I don't want anything happening to you."

"I'm a big boy." Yeah, he is, but still. "I know how to take care of myself." Then his voice turns lower. "And I'm not alone. My cousin is here, remember?"

I smile even if I don't want to. "Don't get hurt," I plead. "Our future is waiting for us."

Preston smiles while he leans down to kiss me softly. "Don't worry about me," he murmurs against my lips before he turns, nods at Damian, and moves to the front door. "Go to the room, Red."

My heart races as I watch the man I'm falling in love with standing in his living room, ready to face the danger.

CHAPTER 13

Preston

That fucker Joseph McCain is standing in my living room as if he were the place's owner. Not the fucker who just sent his nephew to burn half my house down.

"Seems we've got a little issue here, Wolfe."

Old McCain's rough voice rumbles from his broad chest as he steps in front of me. The man is almost sixty, with dark blonde hair going silver at the temples and a thick, salt and pepper beard. Behind him, six other bearded guys follow. All of them dressed in that lumberjack way. Checkered flannels, jeans, and boots.

I don't have to size him up to know if this came down to fists. It'd be an even match. The guy is in pretty good shape for someone his age. I'll give him that.

Zachary comes into view, fuming like a toddler.

"What little issue?" At my question, Zachary's face becomes all flustered, the polar opposite of his uncle's reserved demeanor. "This motherfucker tried to blow my truck up."

Joseph ignores the tantrum his nephew throws, his narrowed gaze on me.

"There's a bit of an issue, as I was saying."

Whatever either of us says next will set the tone of this encounter. We both know it.

I move my head to the cabin behind me. The *issue* is evident right there. "The situation might have something to do with your nephew kindly making renovations to the front of my cabin, as you can see." I turn to level my eyes at Zachary. "I guess he needs some clients for his construction company?"

Joseph smirks as if this situation were giving him some twisted reason to enjoy it.

"Your nephew shot up and tried to burn my cabin down while I was on my patio, Mr. McCain," I say flatly. "I have every right to defend my property…" My gaze is fixed, holding Old McCain's eyes.

Old McCain just keeps smiling that dangerous-looking smile, his eyes crinkling at the corners.

"My land. My rules. You know it."

"I'm bored of this bullshit, Preston." Zachary spits out, taking a step forward. "That woman is here. We want her back."

I look at him with a narrowed gaze, but Old McCain clears his throat before I can say a word. "Wolfe, that woman you're giving safe harbor here stole something from my nephew. It's only fair that he wants it—her—back."

"Mr. McCain, I don't care what wild story your nephew told you, but that's a blatant lie."

The smirk fades from his face as soon as I finish the sentence.

"There is a way to discover the truth," the old man says. "Bring her here."

I don't move, but Old McCain calls one of his minions to walk forward and enter my cabin.

Not happening.

As Damian and I point our guns at his head, he freezes.

"Bring her out, or my guys will bring her out for you." he sighs as all his men level their arms to our chests. "You're playing with fire. Give us what we want, and let's end with this."

"Try it, and just see what happens." A warning leaves my chest. Low and menacing.

He smirks. "Think about this objectively. You're good, but there are eight of us. How do you think this would end, boy?" Again, that fucking smirk remains on his face. I'm about to erase it with my fist. "You have no chance. If you're trying to protect your woman, just do the right thing."

The odds are against us, but the last word hasn't been said. Not yet.

I lose, she loses. And that's not happening.

"Put the guns down," Joseph McCain growls.

"She didn't steal anything."

"That woman isn't telling the truth."

"Let's be honest," I start. "It's not her fault he hired her for his façade company."

"Look, boy…" There's a warning edge to Old McCain's voice as he narrows his eyes at me. But I ignore that as I glare at Zachary, daring him to say a word.

"Not even she understands why you're making a big fuss about a steal. We don't know what you want. Enlighten us."

"Just bring that fucking bitch here out, or I will…"

My gun is up and pointed right at his chest. But then, so are seven other guns pointed directly at my head.

"Shit, Wolfe," Old McCain growls at me. "I'm doing this because you know how much my father loved your grandmother. Otherwise…"

And that's the matter of this old fucking feud because his father was in love with my grandma, and she chose my grandpa instead of that rich spoiled motherfucker.

"You keep her the fuck out of this," I spit back.

Old McCain's jaw tightens. He's close to the breaking point. "You know how much she meant to my father. I'm giving you this chance for her. Drop the gun now."

"What did she steal?"

Zachary swears violently. "She's got a USB that stores important company information."

Another piece of this damned puzzle. But what does it mean?

"A USB? Why is something so small this important to you? What's in there?"

Zachary pales by the second. He's trapped in his own game. Stupid fucker. Old McCain slowly turns to his nephew, his eyes narrowing. We all know a USB is a dangerous weapon. I mean, you can save a lot of information there.

"There better be more than that, Zachary," he growls.

"There are… of course. Uncle Joe, you had me run this side of the business, right? I told you, you just gotta trust me on that, remember?"

Old McCain pauses and then tips his head to some of his guys. The next thing I know I'm on the floor, three guys tackled me, and the others are holding my cousin to the ground.

"Bring her here." Old McCain orders.

The fucking Zachary McCain smirks at me, licking his lips as I roar and try to get those fuckers before they go for London. This war is far from over. We are fighting just another battle. He starts to walk to the hall, then says: "The bedroom, how convenient. I'll be right in there with that whore, and I'll make…"

But something—someone—interrupts him. Standing in the hall is London. She's got a little device in her hand with one of her fingers pushing a button. I know what it is… this girl. She's getting in big trouble.

"I'm ready to blow this cabin away. You know Preston well. The entire place's foundation is full of explosives. The entire mountain is," she bluffs, looking like the hottest badass in the universe. "Let him go. Otherwise, you will be meeting Satan sooner than you expect."

CHAPTER 14

Preston

London is playing with fire. I'm so fucking proud of her, but this shit is dangerous.

"I do believe…," she says, "Preston told you to stay away from this land. Now you're here, threatening us in his living room. You have balls, Mr. McCain."

Old McCain's guys dart their heads around like we're some fancy tennis match, trying to figure out what in the fuck to do. That gives me the chance to get free and stand again. I lock eyes with London, and she winks, flashing me a quick smile before turning her attention back to the McCains.

"I think you're in over your head here, little girl," Old McCain growls at her, his eyes narrowing.

"I'm not the crazy one. Or a thief, for that matter," London says. "Why don't you ask your nephew about the rails?"

"What do you mean?" Zachary is the first to ask.

"The railroads." London swallows hard, but my girl doesn't bugle. "Every one of us knows your construction business is as fake as the wood trade company is. But somehow, you were smart. You're buying supplies with your uncle's money to refurbish the old train railroads to use them for your smuggling business. You're trying to build an empire of your own. You know here in the mountains, there is no law, so you're pretty much free to do whatever you want. You only need to own the land."

"Looks like you found a smart cookie, Preston," Old McCain mutters. He yanks a huge revolver out of his belt, and suddenly, that fucker is pointed right at my head. "You've got seconds to make a point, Miss Moore. I won't hesitate to blow his brain away. Keep that in mind."

"The rails."

"You said that," he warns. "Go straight to the point. I've lost enough time here."

"I was listening inside, Mr. McCain, and your nephew here said that the USB's data was crucial for the company."

I look at my woman, racking my head to figure out where she's going with this and drafting a plan just in case I need to get between her and Old McCain's bullet if it comes to that.

"And?"

"And it got me looking at what I have from Western Woods. Preston's right, all I've got is a lot of information. But that comment gave me the starting point I was waiting for. I believe Zachary forgot to format the USB. There are maps of the railroads in the whole county." Her smart green gaze looks for mine. She's asking me to trust her. She's got this.

I won the jackpot with this girl.

"There are a lot of supply invoices on the USB. The construction company is buying large quantities of steel and wood. That, plus the maps, gave me an idea. The places marked on these maps are possible spots to make stops."

Old McCain's face darkens, the wheels turning in his head as he slowly drags his gaze to his nephew.

"Are you sure?" I ask.

London nods. "I am. Did I tell you my father knew everything about trains? He was an engineer and passionate about everything relating to California's rail network and history."

"Show me." Old McCain orders her.

London's eyes snap to mine, and I nod.

She steps around Zachary with the remote still in her hand, and a finger firmly placed over the little button. In her other hand, she has her cellphone, ready to showcase the information required. Old McCain takes it from her and starts scrolling on the small screen and asking questions that London answers diligently.

"Uncle Joseph, you can't believe her." Zachary whines. "This whore is a crook. She's just trying to trick you by saying…"

"Shut your pipes, Zachary," the older man scolds his nephew.

"Uncle Joe, listen to what I'm saying. This is some bullshit to try and turn you against me…"

"Against you, Zachary?" Old McCain spits.

Joseph McCain is a con but still an intelligent man. He has built an empire in these mountains. Clearly, he understands what his nephew was trying to do here. Some of those rails come directly from Mexico. Others, from Arizona and even Nevada. There is an intricate network of them, from San Bernardino to Big Bear.

"Zachary," he growls, his shoulders tensing and his fists clenching.

"Uncle Joe, if you give me a minute to explain."

"I'm not an idiot, boy. Do you really think I haven't considered this before?"

"Uncle, I was just…"

"Get that ungrateful piece of shit over here." Old McCain barks at his men, his face dark and furious as he turns to his guys.

"Uncle Joe, wait," he pleads. By the look on Old McCain's face, I can tell the man has his mind set.

As some of the guys grab him, Zachary shrieks. They yank him over to his uncle. I glance at Damian for one second before walking right to London's side, engulfing her in my arms and holding her tight like I'm never letting her go. And, I'm not.

Damian clears his throat. "Uh, what the fuck just happened?"

I shoot him a *shut the fuck up look*, and Joseph keeps talking.

"The maps are old but clear. There are several spots marked indicating old train stops. They go across mountains and the border, and once upon a time, I thought they might make a nice alternative to moving goods over the main roads."

By goods, he's not talking about groceries or some illegal wood.

"You're such a smart man, Uncle," Zachary praises.

Old McCain gives him a dark look. "I let it go years ago because it was too expensive. First off, all these old roads are located on private land." McCain's eyes turn to daggers as they narrow at Zachary. "But it seems like you found a way by using my money and resources to attempt to buy the land, and then make a profit with *my* investment."

Zachary grins sheepishly, but his eyes are pleading for mercy. "I swear, Uncle Joe, I was thinking about the future of our family…"

"Sure." The Old man's voice is full of sarcasm. "So, when exactly were you going to tell me about *my* investment? For some reason, I feel like you were going to do this behind my back."

Zachary's face goes white.

"You little piece of shit," he hisses. "Ungrateful motherfucker. All your life, I've treated you like a son, and at the first chance, you do this…"

Zachary moves faster than I'd have ever given him credit for. He snags a gun right from one of Joseph's guys, bringing it up to bear at his uncle, but Damian is faster than everyone else. From my advantage point I see the action almost in slow motion—Matrix movie style—as Damian punches Zachary and knocks him to the ground. Zachary's face is full of blood as he clutches his torso. I bet Damian broke several of his ribs.

Joseph nods, turning to me. "Tell your cousin to calm the fuck down. We're done here." His eyes narrow at his nephew, whimpering on the hardwood floor. This house of mine will need some major renovations after today. "Are we square?"

"Only if you leave London alone," I say quietly, cutting my cousin off as I look at him. "She isn't working for you anymore. She's mine, and she stays here with me. You never come after my land with any sort of scheme again. You honor that, then we're square."

"I can agree to that for letting me know what my nephew was doing behind my back."

I offer him my open hand. "Now we're square."

He shakes it. "Appreciate the info, Miss Moore," he nods at London and turns to leave.

Old McCain gets out of my house and into his truck, his guys dragging Zachary away as they pile into the other vehicles and wheelspin out of the driveway.

"You're so freaking smart. I was standing here terrified and so fucking proud of you," I growl, scooping a shrieking London into my arms. Then taking the remote from within her fingers. She doesn't know what it is. But she will discover the truth soon enough.

"It was a smart move, right?" She giggles, looking a bit smug.

"Don't look so full of yourself, Red," I warn her. She disobeyed me. The time to crimson her little ass is here, and then we are having some fun. "Soon enough, you will be full of me."

She shivers.

"We are leaving," my cousin announces as he saunters past me. "I like her. Take care of this girl and settle the fuck down, Preston." Then Damian smirks. "If you don't marry her, I will."

"The fuck if you are," I spat while giving him the finger and a deadly glare. This woman is mine, and she will be legally tied to me as soon as we reach town.

Once we are alone, I push her into the room. A soft gasp comes out of her sweet lips. "So, what now?"

"I get to love you forever, my little Red."

"I love you, my Mr. Big Bad Wolf."

I kiss her with everything I have. This woman, she's the best thing to have ever happened to me.

CHAPTER 15

London

"You know what this is?" Preston asks me while we both stare at the remote in my hand.

"I have no idea," I reply. To be honest, I just grabbed the first thing that came in handy. I needed a plan, and knowing my Wolfe, having his land full of security measures wasn't that farfetched. The little gadget seemed legit to me, and the McCains believed me, after all.

"Get naked and get in the bed, Red," he orders. His eyes glisten with mischief. He lets me go and stalks to his nightstand, opening the drawer and hides something behind him while I remain anchored to the floor.

What is he planning to do?

"I hope you're feeling adventurous tonight."

"With you," I answer without thinking twice about it. "Always!"

"This will be new for you…" Another warning. "I'll give you a whole new experience."

That intrigues me, and he knows it.

"Get in the bed, Red," he orders again. "On all fours."

A chill makes my entire body tremble. He walks away, I heard him opening a package, then throwing something in the trash before going to the bathroom.

"What should I do with you?" he asks, standing before me. I'm holding the position as he commanded. My heart is hammering so hard the world outside this room has vanished. "You disobeyed me. Again."

"Please," I beg, as his big hand caressed my back softly.

"You don't have any idea what you are asking for."

"Then show me," I say with a bravado I'm not feeling.

He's right. I have no idea what I'm asking for. But I need him, in any way I can have him.

Then the sound of a woosh fills the silence, and his hand cracks my butt.

Fuck, that hurts.

He slaps my ass again, and I close my eyes, embracing the pain.

"I'll be good, I promise." To my surprise, I'm moving my body, looking for more.

"You're fucking fantastic," he praises me. "As you always are, London. You don't have any idea what you do to me. The things running inside my mind every time I look at you. I want my last name on your driver's license and my ring on your finger. I want to have you in this bed every night. Then I want to see your pussy dripping with my cum. I want to smear it on your tits. Fill your mouth with it."

Oh Lord, can a woman die just listening to this man's dirty talk? I'm in flames, and he's barely touched me.

His footsteps cause the floor to creak as he walks around the room, opening a drawer. I bite the pillow and burrow my face in it to silence the moans coming out of my mouth.

When the bed moves, Preston throws two things onto the mattress. A bottle of lubricant, and the other… My eyes are open as saucers.

"Don't make that face, Red," he whispers, his rough hand caressing my behind. "This was your idea."

"M-My idea?" The two words leave my mouth like a stammer.

"The remote, love," he explains. "Seeing you playing that card scared me to death… and made me horny as hell. Plus, I want to punish you."

"Even if I did the right thing?"

I take another look at the vibrator. The thing is made of plastic, and it's massive. Preston laughs. Of course, he thinks it's funny. He won't have that thing deep in his ass. Dickhead.

"This will be intense." No shit. "I'll give you the experience of being completely full. Both your holes, Red."

Oh fuck… will I survive this? The wetness coating my pussy gives me the answer. I want this.

I want this *with him*.

He touches my tight spot with the path of his thumb. "Oh, God." Then he starts to squirt lube on it.

"Take a deep breath." I force myself to do it. "I'm going slow. If this becomes too much for you, just say stop, and I will."

This feels so primitive. So intimate. My skin is burning. Burning for him.

He pushes the vibrator past the tight rim of my ass. "Oh fuck.," I groan while his other hand teasing my clit, making me dizzy. "It's big."

He chuckles. "You have had me there, Red. And I'm bigger."

Yes, that's true. But this feels different. When the monster is seated, he taps the base. Oh, God. The vibrations roll throughout my body.

He keeps touching me in the way he knows I like. In the way only he can.

"Feels good?" Preston still teases me, caressing that spot… then retracting. When I think I'm ready to fly, he anchors me to the ground. If his plan is to torture me, he's succeeding.

"Very," I moan, almost gasping for air.

A second passes, and then another.

"You have me so hard." Preston is naked now; I know it as he strokes the tip of his dick against my wetness. "Are you ready, Red?"

"I'm ready."

"You're so beautiful with the plug in your ass," he says. "You will feel it moving while I'm fucking you."

And he does. His body takes mine in a long deep push. Air leaves my lungs. There is no space for anything else, but him and his implacable rhythm.

His arms are around me, his fingers tweaking my nipples, making them even harder.

"I'm gonna come," I tell him.

"No," he says as he pinches my nipples again. Hard. My pussy gets wetter. This man. "You're gonna hold it. You will wait until I'm ready." He becomes even harder and twitches inside me. He won't last long. My walls tighten around him. We both can play this game. Bring it on, Wolfe!

We are fighting a battle where both of us will win. His hands grip my hip harder. Tomorrow there will be marks all over my skin, and I'll be sore.

"That's it, Red," he praises me again. "Push against me. Make me ride you harder."

So I do.

"Oh, my God!" My orgasm takes me by surprise. It's so big I can't stop it. Not even if I wanted to. I cry out in relief so loud I'm happy we don't have any neighbors.

Preston's entire body tenses as he pushes inside me ruthlessly, and a deep groan rumbles from his chest like thunder.

I fall into the mattress, and he follows me. His weight on me feels comforting and reassuring.

Preston kisses the nape of my neck lazily, while his hands look for mine entwining our fingers together.

"Are you ok, my little Red?"

"I'm barely alive, don't make me talk."

He smiles against my naked shoulder.

"Too intense for you?"

"It was amazing." This time I'm the one smiling. "I want to do it again, but the next time I want you in my…"

Preston laughs hard. "I've created a monster."

I lift my chin even if my face is still on the pillow. "No, you didn't," I counter. "You just freed it."

CHAPTER 16

Preston

Things have worked out very well for us.

London stayed. I won't lie. I was fully prepared to tie her the hell up and keep her with me if she had decided otherwise.

But there was no need. We set up an office in the house where she can get her work done. My wife—did I mention we got married—is helping me to manage my legitimate, and productive wood business.

My other wood is happy with the deal too.

Everything has been peaceful since our little conversation with the McCains. They keep doing their business, and I keep doing mine. The last I've heard, they are doing pretty well. At least Joseph McCain is. Live and let live, as I always say.

As for Zachary? I don't know, and I don't want to know. Zachary pretty much disappeared after that night.

Besides, I've got better things to worry about. The woman in my arms. And the future we are planning together.

And that's exactly what we're working on right at this moment. After coming back from our two-week honeymoon, we decided to start trying to have a baby.

With how often we try, I can guarantee she'll be getting pregnant soon. I groan at the thought of her belly growing round with our child, her breasts filling and swelling.

"You are insatiable, Mr. Big Bad Wolf," she purrs, grinning at me before she kisses me softly. "Not that I'm complaining."

Her little teasing makes me chuckle. "You want to tame me?"

She moves, settling deeper in my arms. "I heard you were the most terrible beast around here," she teases. "Someone has to do the dirty work and keep you in line."

"You looking to apply for the job, Red?" I tease right back.

"Yes."

My entire world is right here. Right in this moment. Right in my arms.

EPILOGUE

London

All my dreams have come true.

We married in Rosarito, Mexico, on the beach behind his grandfather's home during a beautiful sunset. It was a small and intimate affair with just my brother, Preston's grandfather, and his cousins in attendance.

We had our honeymoon in France. We didn't get to truly appreciate the beauty of Paris because we barely left our suite.

Two months after our honeymoon, we found out we were expecting.

When we discovered we were having a little boy, we decided to name him Parker, after Preston's grandfather.

My life is complete. Our journey to get to our happily ever after is what fairy tales are made of.

But our story doesn't end here. For I will always be his little Red, he'll always be my Mr. Big Bad Wolf, and this—this is our big bad love.

THE END

ACKNOWLEDGEMENTS

Special thanks to Ariana, my PA. You know you're a blessing to me. Thank you for all your support. To Britt for making this beautiful cover.

To my bestie, Alexia, thank you for stepping up when I needed it, and run this marathon with me. To Dani for the amazing blurb.

To my Goal Diggers, the best team in *Romancelandia.* Girls, THANK YOU!!

To my husband and daughter, thank you, my loves for your patience and unconditional love. Love you so so much!!

To my friends, the family I chose. Thank you!!

To my readers, for inspiring me every single day.

To God, the strength in every step.

THANK YOU. THANK YOU!!

ABOUT THE AUTHOR

Susana Mohel is a USA Today best-selling author whose stories sizzle like the sunshine in her Southern California mountains.

Her fast-paced, angsty contemporary romance novels transport readers to a world of spunky heroines and hunky heroes who find their way to a happily ever after… with plenty of spiced-up moments along the way.

When she's not writing, Susana can be found wandering the trails along with her husband or creating chaos in her garden.

www.susanamohel.com

Download a FREE book here

Made in the USA
Columbia, SC
24 November 2024